ウェストンが残した
クライマーズ・ブック
KAMIKOCHI ONSENBA CLIMBERS' BOOK.

外国人たちの日本アルプス登山手記

クライマーズ・ブック刊行会編

信濃毎日新聞社

上高地、そして日本の山岳を愛する人たちへ…

穂高連峰をはじめとする北アルプスの山岳や焼岳を目前に見上げる上高地。日本近代登山の父、W・ウェストンはここを拠点に、槍・穂高などへの山行を重ねた。約100年前、この地の温泉場に、欧米からの登山者に書き記してもらうための「クライマーズ・ブック」を残した。

Looking up from Kamikochi toward Mt. Hotaka, Mt. Yakedake and other mountains of the Northern Japanese Alps. It was from this spot that Walter Weston, the father of modern mountaineering in Japan, embarked on a series of climbs to Mt. Hotaka, Mt. Yarigatake, and other peaks. Roughly a century ago, he left a "climbers' book" at the hot springs inn here in which European and American mountaineers could record their journeys.

1913（大正2）年、上高地河童橋でのウェストン夫妻。右側に立つのは山の案内人としてウェストンと親交の厚かった上條嘉門次。編笠を被っているのは妙義山（群馬県）の案内人、根本清蔵。ウェストンは登山靴の上に日本のワラジをはいている。槍沢で以前、登山靴で滑ってびしょ濡れ、泳いで渡ったような記述が著書にある。夫人はスカート姿だが、山に入ると、それがズボンになるというもの。（撮影者は大木操　公益社団法人日本山岳会所蔵）

Weston and his wife at Kappa Bridge in Kamikochi in 1913. Standing at the right is Kamonji Kamijo, a mountain guide with whom Weston developed a close friendship. Wearing the sedge hat is Seizo Nemoto, a guide from Mt. Myogi in Gunma Prefecture. Weston wears Japanese straw sandals over his hiking boots. In his writings he mentions a previous occasion when his boots slipped while hiking through the Yarisawa valley and he ended up soaking wet, swimming across the river. Mrs. Weston is wearing a skirt, which she exchanged for trousers when heading into the mountains. (Photograph by Misao Ohki; collection of the Japanese Alpine Club)

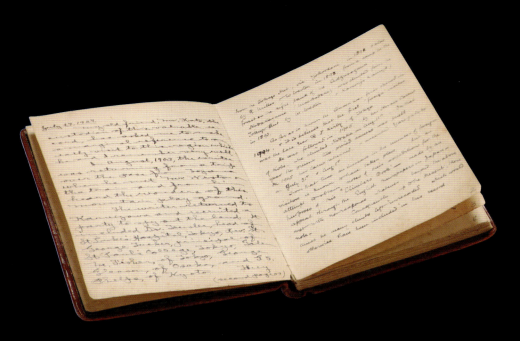

ウェストンが残したクライマーズ・ブック。1914（大正3）年から1972（昭和47）年まで、槍穂高連峰への山行記録など、欧米登山者たちによる50編の記述が記された。冒頭には、ウェストン自身による記述（下写真と次ページ写真）が残されている。

In July 1912 W. Weston returned, after climbing Yari (from a camp near that of 1892) via the Yoko-o-dani & a new route from the Tozuno-goya, over the edge on the ridge & straight up the E face of the peak. After crossing the long & steep snow-slope which forms the source of the Takasegawa. This is an interesting & 'sporting' climb but takes an hour or two longer than the usual route up the S. arête.

A few days later with Kamonji a new way was made to the summit of the highest peak of Hodaka (sometimes known as Takegawa-dake). This is several hundred feet higher than Mae-Hodaka, which is always climbed by travellers coming to ascend Hodaka, who are not made aware of which is actually the highest point of the mountain. The two routes are identical up to the point in the Shiramawa ravine where the latter route turns off to the right. The way to Oku-Hodaka (Takegawa-dake) goes straight on to the end of the long snow slope, (this varies in extent from year to year), ascending by a steep watercourse & a still steeper buttress to reach the great bare rock face forming the upper part of the mountain wall. The top itself is a small rocky point

commanding a magnificent prospect in all directions.

The ascent was made for the most part, in a storm of wind & rain, taking nearly 6 hours up & 4 hours down. It was repeated in fine weather in August 1913 by the same party, including Mrs Weston, the first occasion on which the summit was reached by a lady. The same remark applies to an ascent of Yari by the above mentioned new route up the E face, made during the same month, as well as to the pleasant rock scramble up Kasumi-dake by way of the long gully seen from the Ossen directly opposite. Mae-dake was also climbed on that visit.

In August 1914 a fine expedition was made by Rev. & Mrs Weston from Nakahousa Ossen, in the beautiful valley W. of Akashina, over the top of Otensjo, a fine peak a little NE of Yari on the parallel ridge to the E of the main range. (c 8500 ft) The night was spent at a shelter called the Ninomata hut, on the S. arête of Otensjo, & about 35 minutes below the summit. The first day's walk, including halts takes about 10 or 11 hours.

The second day the ridge is traversed to a

[In October 1913 a party of British naval officers, including Commander Egerton, Lieut Boxton & Sub-Lieut Evans & Barron – all of HMS "Minotaur" visited Kami-kochi. They climbed Yake-dake & also reached within 1000 ft of the summit of Mae Hodaka but the icy condition of the rocks made it necessary to descend.

The mountains at this time were already partly covered with snow.

Early in November Mr Douglas W Freshfield, President of the Royal Geographical Society, Mrs & de Bunsen & Montandon also reached Kamikochi from Shemagima returning instead via Shirahone.]

low gap, W. of Jonendake, & from one point along it fine views of Fuji, Hodaka, Yari &c are obtained.

From this gap, called Nakayama toge, a steep descent is made to the bed of the Ninomata ravine, close to a beautiful lake, formed in 1910 by a fall of rocks from the Akasawa-dake, which dammed up the stream at a most romantic spot.

The Ninomata enters the main valley of the Azusagawa about a ri below the Akasawa hut (on the way to Yari), & thence to the Ossen is a walk of 3 or 4 hours.

This beautiful expedition is highly to be recommended as a picturesque route between Kamikochi & the Matsumoto plain, but the inside of 2 long days should be allowed for it. Also the fact should be borne in mind that especially in hot summers, no water is likely to be found on the route between the Nakayama toge & the neighbourhood of Nakahousa Ossen —

There is excellent accommodation at the latter place, which is well worth a visit for the sake of the splendid valley scenery for the 8 miles or so leading down to Miyashiro on the W. outskirts of the Matsumoto plain.

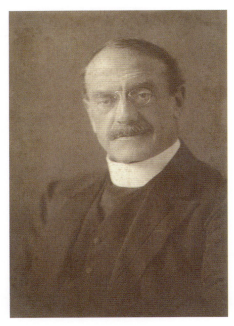

Walter Weston

Kami Kōchi.

August 23rd 1914.

For the use of European & American mountaineers from Rev Walter Weston — English Alpine Club, Hon Memb. Japanese A C, Swiss Alpine Club.

ウェストンがブックへの書き込みを欧米の登山者たちに呼びかけた冒頭のメッセージと、ウェストンの肖像（公益社団法人日本山岳会所蔵）

Above: Portrait of Walter Weston (collection of the Japanese Alpine Club).
Below: Weston's dedication to European and American mountaineers at the start of the book.

『ウェストンが残したクライマーズ・ブック』 刊行に寄せて
外国人たちの日本アルプス登山手記

　日本近代登山の父とも称されるイギリスの宣教師ウォルター・ウェストンは1914（大正3）年夏、生涯で最後となった北アルプス登山のため宿泊した温泉宿「上高地　温泉場」に一冊の厚い日記帳を残しました。表紙に刻まれた文字は『KAMIKOCHI ONSENBA CLIMBERS' BOOK』（「上高地　温泉場　クライマーズ　ブック」）。ウェストンは冒頭で、上高地が既に登山の中心地として人気を集めつつある中、外国人登山者が関心を持ち、有益となるような記録を残す方法が必要であり、滞在客に山行のルートや時間、天候などを記してもらいたい—との趣旨を記しています。

　一部の研究家の間で存在が知られていたクライマーズ・ブックは、内容が広く知られることがないまま、第二次大戦を挟んで書き継がれていきました。署名した人は連名を含めて80人ほどで、英語が中心です。現在は、このブックを引き継いだアルピコグループの上高地ルミエスタホテルが保管し、館内でレプリカを展示しています。

　上高地では毎年6月、ウェストンの功績をたたえて「ウェストン祭」が開かれ、今年が70回目の節目。さらに今年は、初めて迎える国民の祝日「山の日」の8月11日、記念の全国大会が開催されることとなりました。この機会に同書を全訳し、全容を明らかにすることは、日本アルプスを訪れる人々の安全を願ったウェストンの思いを、さらに次の100年へと引き継ぐ足掛かりの一つになると言えるでしょう。本書を通じ、山を愛する人々の輪が国境を越えてさらに広がるよう願ってやみません。

2016年8月
クライマーズ・ブック刊行会

松本市
アルピコグループ
松本市アルプス観光協会
上高地観光旅館組合
北アルプス山小屋友交会
公益社団法人　日本山岳会
信濃毎日新聞社

On the Publication of *The Climbers' Book Left by Walter Weston: Overseas Climbers in the Japanese Alps*

In the summer of 1914, English missionary Walter Weston—known as the father of modern mountaineering in Japan—left a thick notebook at Kamikochi Onsenba, the hot springs inn where he was staying on what would be his final mountaineering trip to the Northern Japanese Alps. The cover was imprinted with the words "Kamikochi Onsenba Climbers' Book." At the beginning of the notebook, Weston wrote that with the growing popularity of Kamikochi as a center for mountaineering—and one of growing interest to overseas climbers—there was a need for some means of recording useful information and that he hoped those staying at the inn would use the book to make note of information such as their climbing routes, times, and the weather.

Although known to a small number of researchers, the climber's book continued to be used even after the Second World War without its content ever reaching the wider world. Including joint signatures, roughly eighty people recorded messages in the book, primarily writing in English. Today the book is kept at the Alpico Group's Kamikochi Lemeiesta Hotel, where a replica is also on display.

The Weston Festival is held in Kamikochi every June to honor Weston's achievements; this milestone year marks the seventieth celebration of the festival. This year also marks the first ever Mountain Day, a newly established national holiday to be commemorated with a national event held in Kamikochi on 11 August. Taking this opportunity to reveal the contents of this book through a complete translation will, we hope, provide a foothold that carries into the next hundred years Weston's desire for the safety of all who visit the Japanese Alps. We hope, too, that this book will contribute to further expanding the community of people around the world who love the mountains.

Committee for the Publication of the Climbers' Book
August 2016

Matsumoto City
Alpico Group
Matsumoto City Alps Kanko
Kamikochi Tourism and Innkeepers' Association
Japan Alpine Lodge Association
The Japanese Alpine Club
The Shinano Mainichi Shimbun

Contents / もくじ

『ウェストンが残したクライマーズ・ブック』
外国人たちの日本アルプス登山手記

『ウェストンが残したクライマーズ・ブック』刊行に寄せて ― 1
   同英訳　On the Publication of *The Climbers' Book Left by Walter Weston : Overseas Climbers in the Japanese Alps* ― 2

はじめに　W・ウェストンが遺した『クライマーズ・ブック』― 4
   同英訳　Introduction : The Climbers' Book Left by Rev. Walter Weston ― 6

ウェストンと『クライマーズ・ブック』― 8
   同英訳　Walter Weston and the Climbers' Book ― 10

ウェストン略歴と日本での山行歴 ― 12

クライマーズ・ブック対訳 ― 13

監修後記 ― 158
   同英訳　Editorial Supervisor's Afterword ― 160

監修・執筆・翻訳スタッフ・編集協力 ― 163

はじめに

W・ウェストンが遺した『クライマーズ・ブック』

ウェストン研究者　三井嘉雄

　明治21年（1888）以来、英国人ウォルター・ウェストンは日本を3回訪れた。いずれも教会団体からの派遣であった。
　来日前にスイスのマッターホルンへ2回も登頂していた山好きのウェストンが、初めて北アルプスを目指したのは明治24年（1891）。英文の『日本旅行案内』で、日本の中央部に高い山があることを知ったからだ。信越線の上田駅から馬車で松本に着いたのは、案内書通りの道筋で、松本の宿、信濃屋旅館も案内書に名があった。
　日本にはまだ登山をする風習がなく、銀も水晶も出ない山に登るということは、人々から不思議がられた時代だった。
　そんな時代、ウェストンが山の旅先での日本人から受けた友情は貴重だった。特に上高地の山案内人であった上條嘉門次、同じく上高地温泉（清水屋とも呼ばれた）の加藤惣吉、後年は妙義山の山案内人であった根本清蔵と心を通わせた信頼関係を築き上げた。
　特に、後に安曇村の村長を務める加藤とは友情を育んだ。ウェストンは、島々から上高地への行き帰り、合わせて11回徳本峠を越している。人類初登頂を成し遂げた南アルプスの鳳凰山の地蔵仏にも感激はしているが、ウェストンにとって上高地こそが絶対的な場所であったに違いない。
　ウェストンを日本びいきにさせた要因は、「日本人のまじめさと、礼儀正しさと、ひなびた田舎の風景に感動したため」と本人が何かに記している。長野県の大町では「すれ違った小学生が自分に挨拶した」と感動していた。

　『クライマーズ・ブック』の表紙には、英活字で「KAMIKOCHI ONSENBA CLIMBARS BOOK」と箔押しされている。この印字は、横浜の山下町10番にあった英字新聞社「ジャパン・ガゼット」のプレス機で押されたものだ。かつてはこのノートの中に、そのことを記したウェストンのメモが入っていた。
　また、このノートは横浜のケリー・ウォルシュ社から購入したものと思われる。英文タイプなど英国製の文房具や、活版印刷機、英文活字などの販売をしていた同社は横浜の本

町通り60番にあり、ジャパン・ガゼット社とはわずか200メートルほどしか離れていない。ちなみに、ウェストンが山行きの参考にしていた英文の『日本旅行案内』改訂第8版の奥付には、印刷が東京牛込区の秀英舎で、発売所は横浜のケリー・ウオルシ商会とある。

　ウェストンは大正3年（1914）、日本で最後となる北アルプスを歩いた。事前に用意した赤表紙のノートを山中でも持ち歩き、上高地の見納めをした後、何回も泊まった上高地温泉を去る時に、それを宿の加藤惣吉に手渡したと思われる。
　ノートの巻頭には、ウェストン自ら「この先ここへ来る外国人登山者に、自分の登山ルート、所要時間、天候などを記してほしい」と記している。いかにも世話好きなウェストンらしい。後日、この温泉に来た人たちのガイド・ブックになるように、さらには登山史にもなるようにと、記録を残してもらうためだった。

　ノートの最初のページの日付けは「1914年8月23日」である。次の24日に上高地温泉を去る予定であったが、当日は雨になったため出発は1日遅れた。ということは、出発予定の前日には日付けを入れて、加藤に渡したという訳だ。ウェストンは後に「今年の上高地への別れは、特に悲しいものであった。これが、われわれにとっては最後の別れになることを知っていたからである」（『日本アルプス再訪』水野勉訳）と書いており、日本を離れがたかったウェストンの心情が読み取れる。
　このノートに書き込みをした人々は、ドイツ語で記入した人も含めると50人を超える。記録の中でも、ガレン・M・フィッシャーの一行による穂高―槍の初縦走の記録は貴重であろう。「これが出版されたら、自分も1冊ほしい」と書き込んだ人もおり、今回の出版に泉下のウェストンも喜んでいることだろう。
　ウェストンは帰英後も、横浜の英字紙『ジャパン・ウィークリー・メイル』を受け取っていた。船便で1カ月遅れではあったが、帰国の年の6月6日に焼岳が大噴火したことも、新聞を読んで知っていた。どんな思いでその記事を読んだことだろうか。

　ウェストン夫妻の墓地は、英国ウィンブルドンのパトニー・ヴェイル墓地にある。墓地番号はBSブロック56番。その墓地を突き止めたのは、嘉門次の曾孫、上條輝夫さんであった。

Introduction

The Climbers' Book Left by Rev. Walter Weston

Yoshio Mitsui
Weston Expert

The Englishman Walter Weston visited Japan three times beginning in 1888, each time sent as a member of a church organization.

An avid mountaineer who had twice summited the Matterhorn in Switzerland prior to his arrival in Japan, Weston first set off for the Northern Alps in 1891 after learning of central Japan's high peaks through *A Handbook for Travellers in Japan*. In reaching Matsumoto by carriage from the Shin'etsu Line's Ueda Station, Weston was following the route described in this handbook, which also noted the name of the inn where he stayed, the Shinano-ya.

There was no custom of mountaineering in Japan at the time; anyone who climbed mountains that yielded neither silver nor crystals was looked upon as something of an eccentric. The friendship Weston received from the Japanese people he met at his mountain destinations, therefore, was invaluable. He developed a close rapport with Kamikochi mountain guide Kamonji Kamijo; with Sokichi Kato of Kamikochi Onsenba (also called Shimizu-ya); and in later years with Mt. Myogi mountain guide Seizo Nemoto.

His friendship with Kato, who would later serve as mayor of Azumi Village, was especially close. Going back and forth between Shimashima and Kamikochi, Weston crossed Tokugo Pass a total of eleven times. Although being the first person ever to climb the obelisk at the peak of Mt. Hoo in the Southern Alps must also have left a deep impression, there seems little doubt that for Weston it was Kamikochi that was the ultimate location.

Weston wrote somewhere that the reason he was so fond of Japan was the earnestness and courtesy of its people, and that he had had been moved by the rustic scenery of the countryside. He was also impressed to have been greeted by the elementary school children he passed while walking in Omachi in Nagano Prefecture.

The title of the *Kamikochi Onsenba Climbers' Book* was stamped in foil on its cover using the press at the Japan Gazette, an English-language newspaper located at No. 10 Yamashita-cho in Yokohama. The book once contained a memo from Weston that recorded this fact.

Weston is believed to have purchased the notebook at Kelly & Walsh Ltd. in Yokohama. Located at Motomachi No. 60, this shop sold British typewriters and stationery, letterpress equipment, and printing type and was located just 200 meters from the offices of the Japan Gazette. The colophon in the eighth revised edition (1907) of *A Handbook for Travellers in Japan*, a title Weston continued to refer to when planning his trips to the mountains, notes that it was printed by Shueisha of Ushigome-ku in Tokyo and sold by Kelly & Walsh Ltd. of Yokohama.

During Weston's last mountaineering trip to the Northern Japanese Alps in 1914, he carried with him the red-bound notebook that he had prepared in advance. After seeing Kamikochi for the final time, he is believed to have given it to Sokichi Kato at Kamikochi Onsenba, where he had stayed so many times before, upon his departure

At the beginning of the book, Weston wrote that he hoped foreign travelers would, in the future, use the book to make note of the routes they had taken, the time required, the weather experienced, and other details. Ever looking for ways to help others, he seems to have wanted people to leave a record of their journeys such that the notebook would serve as a guide for later visitors to the area and even as part of mountaineering history.

The first entry in the notebook is dated 23 August 1914. Weston had intended to leave Kamikochi Onsenba the following morning but as the 24th brought rain his departure was postponed by one day. In other words, he dated the book and gave it to Kato on the day prior to his intended departure. In *The Playground of the Far East* (1918) Weston later wrote, suggesting his reluctance to leave Japan, "Our 'good-bye' to Kamikochi this year was one of special sadness, for we knew it was to be our final farewell."

More than fifty people left messages in the notebook, some writing in German. The record left by Galen M. Fisher of his party's first traverse of the route from Hotaka to Yari is particularly valuable. One message even records the writer's desire to have a copy of the notebook, and one imagines that Weston, too, must be pleased that it is now being published.

After returning to England, Weston continued to receive the Japan Weekly Mail, an English-language newspaper from Yokohama. Issues arrived by ship a month late, and it was through this medium that Weston learned of the eruption of Mt. Yakedake on 6 June in the year of his return. I wonder how he must have felt as he read the article.

Weston and his wife are buried at Putney Vale Cemetery in Wimbledon, at number 56 in block BS. It was Kamonji's great-grandson Teruo Kamijo who traced the location.

ウェストンと『クライマーズ・ブック』

⛏ ウォルター・ウェストン （Walter Weston 1861-1940）

　イギリスの宣教師として、1888（明治21）年に初来日。1914（大正3）年までに計3回、日本を訪れた。延べ11年余の滞在の間、日本アルプスをはじめ日本各地の山岳に登る。その見聞録を記した著書『日本アルプスの登山と探検』を1896（明治29）年に母国英国で出版、日本アルプスなどの山々や当時の風習を世界に紹介した。この本を目にした岡野金次郎や小島烏水との出会いが日本山岳会創設のきっかけにもなった。これらの功績から、ウェストンは「日本近代登山の父」とも呼ばれる。

　日本滞在で初めてのアルプス登山は1891（明治24）年、上高地へ入り、槍ヶ岳をめざした。この時は悪天候のため、登頂はならなかったが、翌年の92（同25）年に槍ヶ岳に登頂。93（同26）年には立山などに登り、安曇村出身の猟師だった上條嘉門次の案内で前穂高岳に登頂。山案内人として厚い信頼を寄せた嘉門次とは、長く交流が続いた。94（同27）年には白馬岳、笠ケ岳、常念岳に登った。2度目の来日となった1902（明治35）年以降の山行では、しばしばフランセス夫人も同伴している。1915（大正4）年に日本を離れてからも、日本を紹介する講演で英国各地を回ったり、秩父宮様のスイスでの登山に協力した。

　長野県松本市の上高地では、1937（昭和12）年8月26日、梓川河畔の岩壁にウェストン顕彰のレリーフが設置された。1947（昭和22）年から「上高地を"再発見"したウォルター・ウェストン」を記念して、毎年「ウェストン祭」が開かれている。

上高地の梓川河畔にある
ウェストンのレリーフ

The Weston relief along the banks of the Azusa River.

⛏ クライマーズ・ブック （『KAMIKOCHI ONSENBA CLIMBERS' BOOK』）

　赤ワイン色、革張りの『KAMIKOCHI ONSENBA CLIMBERS' BOOK』はA5判、全138ページ。ウォルター・ウェストンの署名で1914（大正3）年8月23日を記入最初の日付とし、それ以降、1972（昭和47）年9月11日まで、上高地を訪れた各国の登山者によって山行記録や登山道の様子、当日の天候、槍・穂高連峰をはじめ日本アルプスの印象などが自由に書き込まれている。1915（大正4）年の焼岳噴火時と直後の様子を詳細に記した貴重な記述も残る。

　タイトルにある「ONSENBA（温泉場）」は、上高地に開かれた温泉宿泊施設の名称に由来する。ウェストンはこの温泉場を定宿とし、日本滞在の最後に残したのが「クライマーズ・ブック」。その冒頭、1ページから計7ページ分、「こうした記録は単に興味深いだけでなく、有益な情報にもなるだろう。この温泉場に滞在する欧米の旅行者には、登山ルートや所要時間、天候などに関するその時々の詳細な情報を簡潔かつ明確に記されたい」旨の記述が残る。それに続く記述は主語が「私」などの一人称ではなく、ウェストン本人の名前が出てくるが、生前に残された筆跡から自身の記述と認められる。

　ブックは、ウェストンが日本アルプスに足を運んだ明治時代中期から定宿にしていた旅館の主人で、温泉場の運営を任されていた加藤惣吉氏（元安曇村長）に託されたとされる。欧米などからの登山者らによる山行録など50編の記述が記された。ブックは現在、上高地の梓川河畔にあるアルピコグループのホテル「上高地ルミエスタホテル」に保管され、フロントで複製を公開している。

上高地ルミエスタホテルで公開している
クライマーズ・ブック（複製）

A replica of the climbers' book is shown to the public at the Kamikochi Lemeiesta Hotel.

Walter Weston and the Climbers' Book

⛏ Who was Walter Weston?

Walter Weston first came to Japan as an English missionary in 1888. He arrived for his third and final visit in 1914. During the total of eleven years that he spent in Japan he frequently climbed mountains in the Japanese Alps and elsewhere around the country. The account of his travels published in his native England in 1896, *Mountaineering and Exploration in the Japanese Alps*, introduced the mountains of Japan and the country's customs of the day to the world. Weston's meeting with Kinjiro Okano and Usui Kojima, who had seen this book, led to the establishment of the Japanese Alpine Club. It is for these contributions that Weston is known as the father of modern mountaineering in Japan.

Weston's first climb in the Japanese Alps took place in 1891 when he came in through Kamikochi aiming for Mt. Yarigatake. Poor weather prevented him from summiting on that occasion but he did succeed in reaching the peak the following year. In 1893 he climbed Mt. Tateyama and, guided by a hunter from Azumi Village named Kamonji Kamijo, made the summit of Mt. Maehotaka. Weston found Kamonji to be a trusted guide and the two maintained a long relationship. In 1894 he climbed Mt. Shirouma, Mt. Kasadake and Mt. Jonen. Beginning with his second trip to Japan that started in 1902, Weston was often accompanied in the mountains by his wife Frances. After leaving Japan for the final time in 1915, Weston toured England giving lectures about Japan and provided support when Prince Chichibu went mountain climbing in Switzerland.

On 26 August 1937 a commemorative relief of Weston was installed on a rock face along the banks of the Azusa River in Kamikochi. Since 1947, the annual Weston Festival has been held to honor Weston as the man who "rediscovered" Kamikochi.

⛰ The Climbers' Book

Bound in wine-red leather, the *Kamikochi Onsenba Climbers' Book* is an A5 format notebook containing 138 pages. The first entry, signed by Walter Weston, was recorded on 23 August 1914, after which mountaineers visiting Kamikochi from countries around the world continued to write freely about their climbs, the condition of the trails, the weather, and their impressions of the Yari–Hotaka Range and the Japanese Alps up until 11 September 1972. It also includes a valuable and detailed account of the eruption of Mt. Yakedake in 1915 and its immediate aftermath.

The "Kamikochi Onsenba" in the title was the name of the hot springs inn in Kamikochi where Weston frequently stayed, and where he left the climbers' book when he said farewell to Japan. The first entry in the book, running seven pages, begins, "It is hoped that such a record will prove not only of interest but also of useful information, and it is requested that those details as to routes, times, weather, etc. may be briefly and clearly noted by those European and American travellers who stay at the Onsen from time to time." The text that follows is written in the third person rather than the first, referring often to "Mr. Weston," but a comparison of handwriting samples known to be Weston's confirms this record to be his own.

Weston is thought to have entrusted the book to Sokichi Kato, an old friend who managed Kamikochi Onsenba and later served as mayor of Azumi Village. It contains more than fifty climbing records and other messages left by mountaineers from Europe, the United States, and elsewhere. Today the book is kept at the Alpico Group's Kamikochi Lemeiesta Hotel along the Azusa River in Kamikochi, where a replica is available at the reception desk for viewing by the public.

ウェストン略歴と日本での山行歴

1861（文久元）			12月25日、イングランド中部のダービーで生まれる
1886（明治19）	24歳		スイスのアルプスで本格的な登山を始める
1887（明治20）	25歳		牧師となる
1888（明治21）	26歳		初来日（大阪入り）、初任地の熊本へ
1890（明治23）	28歳		富士山、阿蘇山、祖母山、桜島、霧島山、日光白根山
1891（明治24）	29歳		浅間山、槍ヶ岳（登頂断念）、御嶽山、木曽駒ケ岳、富士宝永山
1892（明治25）	30歳		富士山、乗鞍岳、槍ヶ岳、赤石岳
1893（明治26）	31歳		恵那山、富士山、針ノ木峠、立山、前穂高岳（案内の上條嘉門次と出会う）
1894（明治27）	32歳		白馬岳、笠ケ岳、焼岳、常念岳、御嶽山。英国に帰国
1896（明治29）	34歳		『日本アルプスの登山と探検』出版（英国で著す）
1902（明治35）	40歳		フランセス・エミリーと結婚。二度目の来日、富士山、北岳
1903（明治36）	41歳		甲斐駒ケ岳。岡野金次郎、小島烏水と出会う
1904（明治37）	42歳		金峰山、鳳凰山のオベリスク、北岳、間ノ岳、仙丈ケ岳、八ヶ岳、富士山、戸隠山、高妻山、妙高山
1905（明治38）	43歳		帰国。小島烏水に山岳会設立を勧める。小島らが「山岳会」設立（09年に「日本山岳会」の名称に）
1910（明治43）	48歳		日本山岳会の名誉会員
1911（明治44）	49歳		12月、三度目の来日
1912（明治45／大正元）	50歳		妙義山、有明山、燕岳、槍ヶ岳、奥穂高岳
1913（大正2）	51歳		妙義山、槍ヶ岳、焼岳、霞沢岳、奥穂高岳、白馬岳
1914（大正3）	52歳		立山、針ノ木峠、燕岳、大天井岳、富士山 8月、上高地の温泉宿に『クライマーズ・ブック』を備える
1915（大正4）	53歳		1月帰国
1918（大正7）	56歳		『極東の遊歩場』出版（英国で著す）
1925（大正14）	63歳		『知られざる日本を旅して』出版（英国で著す）
1926（大正15／昭和元）	64歳		秩父宮様のスイス・アルプス登山に協力
1937（昭和12）	75歳		フランセス夫人死去 8月、日本山岳会が上高地に顕彰レリーフ設置
1940（昭和15）	78歳		死去

クライマーズ・ブック
対　訳

対訳について ─────────

◆ 左側のページに原文（主に英語。ほかにフランス語、ドイツ語、漢詩あり）、右側のページに日本語訳文を置いた。

◆ 右側の日本語訳文には、必要に応じて山岳ジャーナリスト菊地俊朗氏による「注釈」を付けた。原文筆者の「思い込み」の補正や、記述の山岳史における意味などを補完した。（ただし，明朝体の注釈は編集部による）

◆ 掲載順は、①ノート原本の記載順②書かれた日付③書かれている内容（出来事）の日付─から判断した。原本の記載順番は不規則なため、編集部の判断で入れ替えた箇所もある。なお、文章冒頭の帯部分にある年／月は、原則「書かれた日」としたが、分からない場合は内容から取った箇所もある。

◆ 本書における読みやすさを重視し、原文は手書きの体裁を無視して原則「左寄せ」とした。また、必要に応じて行空けや改行を調整した。

◆ 原文（手書き）には、判読が困難な文字や言葉もあり、推測や省略をして活字化、翻訳した部分もある。判読できない文字は「＊」で示した。

◆ 固有名詞等の読み方で、原文の中で筆者が記述しながら、現在はそう読まなかったり、筆者が間違っている場合は、原文の記述内容をカタカナのルビで載せた。

◆ 下線は、筆者が記述しているものを再現し、訳文にも連動させた。

◆ 原文と和文の位置が左右でずれるため、同じ段落の位置を示すマーク（★♥♠◆♣）を適宜段落の最初に入れた。

Kamikochi

August 23rd 1914

For the use of European & American mountaineers
from Rev. Walter Weston.

English Alpine Club
Hon. Memb. Japanese AC
Swiss Alpine Club

クライマーズ・ブック対訳

上高地

1914年8月23日

欧米の登山家に役立つように
ウォルター・ウェストン牧師

英国山岳会
日本山岳会名誉会員
スイス山岳会

The growing popularity of Kamikochi as a centre for mountaineering in this part of the Japanese Alps suggests, as in the case of other Alpine regions, the desirability of establishing some means of recording expeditions of interest to 'foreign' climbers who are now visiting it in growing numbers.

It is hoped that such a record will prove not only of interest but also of useful information, & it is requested that those details as to routes, times, weather, &c. may be briefly & clearly noted by those European & American travellers who stay at the Onsen from time to time.

The first known foreign visitors to the spot were the Rev. Walter Weston, & the Rev. H.J. Hamilton, in 1894, on their way from the first ascent of Kasa-dake from Gamada. A record of this & other expeditions in this region (including ascents of Yarigatake & Hodakayama, &c.) is to be found in "Mountaineering in the Japanese Alps" by the former traveler. At that time there were no shelters to be had, beyond the Tokugo hut, & the tracks were few & indistinct.

Yarigatake was climbed by H.W. Belcher & W. Weston from the Tokugo Hut, via Yokoodani, in 1891 & also by R. Miller & W. Weston in 1892 from a camp in the forest on the right bank of Adzusagawa.

★ Hodakayama (Maehodaka) was climbed from the Tokugo hut by W. Weston (& Kamonji Kamijō) in 1893.

As far as is known the Onsen was first opened in 1904, & it is believed that the first 'foreign' visitor was the late Mr. R.J. Kirby, of Tokyo.

He was followed in 1905 by Mr. Horace Carew of Kobe, who climbed Hodaka on Aug 11th. In that year the present two-storied annex was built. In 1905 Mr. Carew returned & ascended Yarigatake on July 31st & Aug. 1st.

From that time, an increase in the number of foreign visitors is known to have taken place but an attempt to obtain notes of their expeditions for the purposes of this "Climbers' Book" — made by an appeal through the English newspapers in Japan — met with no response whatever beyond the above

クライマーズ・ブック対訳

1914.8（前ページからの続き）※

上高地は日本アルプスの登山の中心地として人気の高まりを見せている。そこで、他の山岳地帯と同じように上高地でも、急増する「外国人」登山者が関心を持つような登山記録を残す何らかの方法を築くことが望まれる。

こうした記録は単に興味深いだけでなく、有益な情報にもなるだろう。この温泉場に滞在する欧米の旅行者には、登山ルートや所要時間、天候などに関するその時々の詳細な情報を簡潔かつ明確に記されたい。

当地を最初に訪れた外国人は、1894年に蒲田（ガマダ）からの笠ヶ岳（カサダケ）初登攀①の帰り道に立ち寄ったウォルター・ウェストン牧師とH・J・ハミルトン牧師とされている。そのときの登山をはじめ、この地域の山々（槍ヶ岳や穂高山（ホダカヤマ））などを登ったときの記録は、ウォルター・ウェストン牧師の『日本アルプスの登山と探検』②に見ることができる。当時、徳本（とくごう）の小屋③以外に利用できる避難所は一切なく、登山道もそれとはっきり分かるものはほとんどなかった。

槍ヶ岳には、1891年にH・W・ベルチャーとW・ウェストンが徳本小屋から横尾谷経由で④、また、1892年にはR・ミラーとW・ウェストンが梓川右岸の森林にあるキャンプ地から登った。

★ 穂高山（前穂高）は1893年にW・ウェストン（と上條嘉門次）が徳本の小屋から登攀している。

上高地温泉の開湯は1904年⑤というのが通説で、初の「外国人」利用者は東京からきた故R・J・カービー氏だったと考えられている。

その後に利用したのは1905年に神戸からきたホレス・カルー氏だ。8月11日に穂高に登っている。同年、現存する2階建ての別棟が建設された。カルー氏は1905年に再度上高地に戻り、7月31日から8月1日にかけて槍ヶ岳に登って

※この文章は末尾に署名がないが、ウォルター・ウェストンの署名がある前ページと同じ筆跡で書かれている。

①笠ヶ岳は大永年間（1521〜27）に道泉、ついで円空、南裔ら修験者の登山が伝えられ、播隆の三度の登頂はよく知られる。

②正式な英文タイトルは「Mountaineering and Exploration in the Japanese Alps」。

③徳本の小屋は、現在の峠の小屋ではない。白沢の梓川合流点付近にあった農商務省山林局の管理小屋。

④ウェストンの1回目の槍登山（1891）は、横尾から左折して横尾本谷→天狗原ルートをとった、雨天で登頂できず、翌年、梓川ルートで登頂。

⑤上高地温泉は文政期（1818〜29）に飛州新道を開いた岩岡伴次郎が湯屋を開業。幕末まで営業。1904年は青柳堯次郎による温泉会社の創立年。

note. Consequently, up to the present, there must be many climbs left unrecorded which would otherwise have been included in this record.

♥ In Aug 1912, Mr. Weston returned, after climbing Yari (from a camp near that of 1892) via the Yokoōdani & a new route from the Bozugoya over the ridge on the ridge & straight up the E face of the peak, after crossing the long & steep snow slope which forms the source of the Takasegawa. This is an interesting & 'sporting' climb but takes an hour or two longer than the usual route up the S. arête.

A few days later with Kamonji, a new way was made to the summit of the <u>highest</u> peak of Hodaka (sometimes known as Takegawadake). This is several hundred feet higher than <u>Mae</u>-Hodaka, which is always climbed by travellers coming to ascend 'Hodaka' who are not made aware of which <u>is</u> actually the highest point of the mountain. The two routes are identical up to the point in the Shirasawa ravine where the latter route turns off to the right. The way to Oku Hodaka (Takegawa Dake) goes straight on to the end of the long snow slope (this varies in extent from year to year), ascending by a steep watercourse & a still steeper buttress to reach the great bare rock face forming the upper part of the mountain wall. The top itself is a small rocky point commanding a magnificent prospect in all directions.

This ascent was made, for the most part, in a storm of wind & rain, taking nearly 6 hours up & 4 hours down. It was repeated, in fine weather, in August 1913, by the same party including Mrs. Weston, the first occasion on which the summit was reached by a lady. The same remark applies to an ascent of Yari by the above mentioned new route up the E face, made during the same month, as well as to the pleasant rock scramble up Kasumi dake by way of the long gully seen from the Onsen directly opposite. Yakedake was also climbed on that visit.

In October 1913 a party of British naval officers, including Commander Egerton, Lieut. Buxton & Sub-Lieuts. Evans & Bavin, all of HMS "Minotaur," visited Kamikochi. They climbed Yakedake, & also reached within 1000 ft of the summit of Mae Hodaka, but the icy condition of the rocks made it

いる。

　それからというもの外国人旅行者の数が増したことは周知の事実だが、「クライマーズ・ブック」のために登山記録を集めようという動きはあったものの（日本の英字新聞で声掛けが行われた）、先に述べた内容以外、情報は一切得られなかった。そのため、ここに記録が残されることなく終わった登山が、現在にいたるまで数多くあるに違いない。

♥　1912年8月、ウェストン氏は槍に登攀し（1892年のキャンプ地付近で野営）、上高地に戻る。このときは、横尾谷経由の、坊主小屋を通る新ルートで登攀した。高瀬川の水源となる長く険しい雪渓を横切り⑥、尾根を縦走、東面からまっすぐ槍の穂先を目指している。これはおもしろくて「楽しめる」登山だが、南側のやせ尾根を登るいつものルートよりも1時間から2時間長くかかる。

　数日後、上條嘉門次とともに、穂高最高峰（岳川岳とも呼ばれる）の山頂へと続く新しいルートを作った。この山頂は前穂高より100m以上高い。「穂高(ホダカ)」を登りに来た登山者は必ず前穂高に登るが、実はどの山が最高峰なのか分かっていないのだ。二つのルートは白沢(しらさわ)⑧の出合まで全く同じだが、前穂高へのルートはこの出合で右に曲がる。奥穂高（岳川岳）へは、雪をかぶった長い斜面をそのまま最後まで進む（雪の範囲は年によって違いがある）。険しい水流とさらに急峻(きゅうしゅん)なバットレス沿いを登ると、見事な岩肌を見せる山壁上部にたどり着く。頂はごつごつした鋭鋒で、見渡す限り絶景が広がる。

　このときの登攀ではほとんどの行程が嵐で、登頂にほぼ6時間、下山には4時間かかった。1913年8月、好天に恵まれ、初登頂のメンバーにウェストン夫人を加えたパーティーで再び山頂を目指す。女性が登頂した初めてのケースだ⑨。同じ8月には、新ルートで達成した前述の槍東壁登攀に加えて、上高地温泉の真正面に見える長い岩溝(ガリー)を経由した、霞岳の快

⑥ウェストンの3回目は、夫人とともに槍沢上部から現・大槍ヒュッテ付近の東鎌尾根に登り、高瀬川源流上部の天上沢の雪渓をトラバースしているが、槍ヶ岳山荘の穂苅貞雄氏は天上沢から登ったわけではない、としている。

⑦分かりにくい説明だが、岳沢から直接、バリエーションルートで奥穂に登った。鵜殿正雄らが穂高ー槍を縦走したのは1909年。

⑧「白沢」は不明。

⑨北アでは女性の登山は限られていたが、富士山では幕末から、立山では明治初期から。長野、松本高女は明治35年から学校登山を実施している。

クライマーズ・ブック対訳

necessary to descend.

♠ The mountains at this time were already partly covered with snow.

Early in November Mr. Douglas W. Freshfield, President of the Royal Geographical Society, & Mr. E. de Bunsen of the Embassy also reached Kamikochi from Shimajima returning thither via Shirahone.

In August 1914, a fine expedition was made by Mr. & Mrs. Weston from Nakabusa Onsen, in the beautiful valley W. of Akashina, over the top of Ōtenjō, a fine peak a little NE of Yari on the parallel ridge to the E of the main range.

The night was spent at a shelter called the Ninomata hut (c.8500ft) on the S. arête of Ōtenjō, & about 35 minutes below the summit. The first day's walk, including halts takes about 10 or 11 hours.

The second day the ridge is traversed to a low gap, W. of Jōnendake, & from one point along it fine views of Fuji, Hodaka, Yari &c. are obtained.

From this gap, called Nakayama toge, a steep descent is made to the bed of the Ninomata ravine, close to a beautiful lake, formed in 1910, by a fall of rocks from the Akasawa-dake, which dammed up the stream at a most romantic spot.

♠ The Ninomata enters the scenic valley of the Adzusa gawa about a ri below the Akasawa hut (on the way to Yari), thence to the Onsen is a walk of 3 or 4 hours.

This beautiful expedition is highly to be recommended as a picturesque route between Kamikochi & the Matsumoto plain, but the inside of 2 long days should be allowed for it. Also the fact should be borne in mind that, especially in hot summers, no water is likely to be found on the route between the Nakayama toge & the neighbourhood of Nakabusa Onsen.

♣ There is excellent accommodation at the latter place, which is well worth a visit for the sake of the splendid valley scenery for the 8 miles or so leading down to Miyashiro on the W. outskirts of the Matsumoto plain.

適な岩登りにも成功しているが、それもまた女性初の登頂になる。そのときの上高地滞在では焼岳にも登った。

　1913年10月、イガートン中佐、バクストン大尉、エヴァンス、ベイヴィン両中尉など軍艦マイノーターに乗艦していた英国海軍士官一行が上高地を訪れる。焼岳に登頂、また、前穂高には山頂まであと約300mという地点まで登攀したが、岩肌が凍結しており、下山を余儀なくされた。

♠　このとき、山の一部は既に雪をかぶっていた。

　11月上旬には、王立地理学会会長のダグラス・W・フレッシュフィールド氏、英国大使館のE・デ＝ブンゼン氏が島々から上高地に入り、白骨経由で島々に戻った。

　1914年8月、ウェストン夫妻が明科西部の美しい谷にある中房温泉から登山を楽しみ、大天井岳の山頂を越えた。この見事な頂は槍の少し北東、連峰主稜線（りょうせん）の東側に並行して連なる尾根に位置する。

　夜は、大天井の南アレートの、山頂から35分ほど下ったところにある二ノ俣小屋（約2,590m）という避難小屋⑩で明かした。初日の登山には休憩も含め、10時間か11時間ほどかかっている。

　2日目は、尾根を常念岳の西側にある鞍部（あんぶ）までトラバースする。谷に沿って進む道中、富士や穂高、槍といった山々のすばらしい眺望が眼前に広がる。

　この中山峠⑪と呼ばれる鞍部から険しい下りを進むと、二ノ俣谷の谷底にたどり着く。近くにある美しい池は、赤沢岳の落盤で1910年にできたものである。景色が特に美しい場所で、川の流れがせき止められたのだ。

◆　二ノ俣の先には、（槍へのルートにある）赤沢小屋の1里ほど下を流れる梓川の風光明媚（めいび）な谷が続く。そこから上高地温泉までは徒歩で3、4時間だ。

　この美しい行程は、上高地と松本平を結ぶ、まるで絵のようなルートとして特にお薦めだ。だが、丸2日はかかると見

クライマーズ・ブック対訳

⑩長野県は増えてきた登山者対策に大正10年前後、県内10ヵ所に避難用石室を設けた。その一つが東天井岳にあった。

⑪今は廃道になったが、喜作新道整備以前の槍ヶ岳への登路は、東天井から中山峠越えで梓川の二ノ俣合流点に出て槍沢を登った。
赤沢岳✗→赤沢山○

Impressions de Voyage à Kamikochi

Kamikochi, encore peu connu des Européens, est assurément un lieu de villégiature plein de charmes pour quiconque, fatigué de la tyrannie du monde , aime la solitude, le calme, l'air pur des montagnes et désire se reposer au milieu de paysages variés , ou gais ou tristes, ou jolis ou même sinistres.

Aime-t-on les hauts sommets, les ascensions quelque peu pénibles et fatigantes ? L'Hotaka-Dake, haute montagne à un kilomètre de Kamikochi, facile à gravir en une journée et le Yari-ga-take qui exige deux jours d'excursion feront jouir l'alpiniste d'un vaste panorama sur les montagnes de Hida et de l'Echu à l'Ouest et sur le radieux Fuji-yama au Sud Mais c'est surtout le volcan Yake-ga-také qui est le plus grand attrait de Kamikochi.

★ Portant bien son nom de « Mont brulé », ce pic, qui éteint depuis des siècles a éclaté de nouveau en 1902, a probablement l'un des plus curieux cratères des nombreux volcans du Japon.

En général les cratères ont la forme circulaire d'un entonnoir aux parois plus ou moins éboulées, le Yake-ga-take au contraire est une longue et profonde crevasse aux parois à pic comme une falaise qui vomit sans cesse

ておいた方がよい。また、ことに夏の暑い時期、中山峠と中房温泉一帯を結ぶルートでは水場が見つけられない可能性が高いので、留意すること。

♣ 中房温泉には優れた宿があり、松本平西側の宮城へと続く約13kmは特に谷の風景がすばらしく、訪れるだけの価値がある。

1914.8（フランス語）

上高地紀行

　まだ、ヨーロッパの人々にあまり知られていない上高地は魅力にあふれた保養地です。上高地は、時に美しい自然が、時に荒々しい自然が、乱れた世の中に疲弊した人々の心を癒やし、また、山の澄んだ空気や静けさ、孤独を求める人々の心を満足させてくれるに違いありません。

　本格的な登山がお好みであれば、1kmしか離れていない穂高岳は日帰りで簡単に登れます①。また、2日あれば、堂々たる槍ヶ岳の山頂から飛騨や富山の山々、光り輝く富士山など雄大なパノラマが、登山者の目を楽しませてくれます。しかしながら、上高地の最高の見どころは何と言っても、焼岳（ヤケガタケ）でしょう。

★ その名は、直訳で「焼けた山」という意味になりますので、火山にぴったりなネーミングといえます。数世紀に渡って眠っていたその山は、1902年新たに噴火しました②。日本列島に点在する数多くの火山に比べて、火口が不思議な形をしています。

　一般的に火山の火口は円形なものがほとんどですが、なぜ

①叙情的な上高地の印象訳なので、実情との開きがあるのでは。前穂高でも、一般登山者に日帰りは厳しい。

②焼岳周辺は太古から火山活動が続く。20世紀に入って活発になったが、大正池を生んだ大噴火は1915年。

des flots de fumée sulfureuse

♥ Si le vent est favorable, on peut par instants apercevoir le fond même du cratère et les rochers d'un jaune éclatant par le soufre dont ils sont couverts.

Tout le sommet de cette montagne est en feu, partout des solfatares, partout des trous d'où s'échappe une fumée suffocante. On a la sensation de marcher sur une chaudière souterraine. Paysage sinistre et impressionnant.

Même la montagne voisine, séparée du volcan par le col qui conduit au village de Garadda est brûlante; il suffit d'enfoncer sa canne dans le sol pour qu'aussitôt prenne naissance un solfatare Il semble bien que le volcan est à la veille d'une nouvelle éruption

En partant de grand matin, cette ascension peut se faire sans trop de fatigue en une demi-journée.

♠ Au retour de toutes ces excursions, le touriste a l'agréable satisfaction de pouvoir prendre un bain d'eau thermale, qui sort d'un rocher à quelques mètres de l'hôtel.

Cette eau chaude coule claire et limpide d'un jet continu, dans une immense baignoire remarquable par son extrême propreté. Voilà certes un précieux avantage qui fait vite oublier la fatigue d'une pénible ascension

Enfin pour charmer ses loisirs et chasser l'ennui, on peut se distraire en péchant la truite, qui abonde dans le torrent Atsusa , au bord duquel est bâti l'hôtel de Kamikochi, ou en se promenant dans le merveilleux chemin qui longe ce torrent. Pendant plus de deux lieues on marche sous un dôme de verdure, qui donne l'illusion d'une promenade dans un parc, comme on en trouve dans aucune capitale ni dans aucun jardin princier.

Kamikochi, 29 aout 1914
L. Drouart de Lézey

か焼岳の火口は長方形で、険しい谷のごとく、深い地割れのような姿を見せ、その奥底からは絶えず大量な硫黄酸ガスを吐き出しています。

③「長方形」の縦列火口は伊豆諸島など他にもある。

♥ 順風に恵まれたら、一瞬、鮮やかに黄色く染まった大地の胎内を垣間見ることができます。

山頂一帯が火に包まれ、あちこちで無数の穴から息詰まるような煙を吹き出しています。大変印象的な火山です。

峠を越えた隣の山でさえ、自分のつえを土に打ち込むだけで、硫気孔が生まれるぐらいですから、焼岳はいつ再び噴火してもおかしくないでしょう。

朝早く出発すれば、半日ぐらいで焼岳の登山ができます。

♠ 山歩きの後は、ホテルのすぐ近くから湧き出ている温泉につかるのが、最高の楽しみです。

お湯は透明で、絶えず豊富な湯が湯船に注がれています。この湯船はまた、びっくりするほど大きくて、大変清潔です。この温泉は登山の疲れを癒やしてくれる貴重なものです。

平凡な生活の倦怠感を紛らわせるには、ホテルの横を流れる梓川でニジマスを釣ることがおすすめです。また、小川に沿ったすてきな小道を歩くこともしかり。2里（約8km）ほどにわたる緑のトンネルのような散歩道は、まるで幻想の世界。世界中のどんな宮殿の庭園にもかなわないほど……。

上高地、
1914年8月29日
ルシアン・ドルアン・デ・レゼー

Hodakayama May, 1915

On Friday, May 21st, we crossed the Tokugo Toge, which was thickly covered with snow for the last ri, & a perfectly clear day gave us a magnificent view of Hodakayama from the summit. Our intention was to return to Shimashima via Kamikochi & Shirahone, but this sight decided us to intervene an attempt at climbing Hodakayama.

Kamikochi Onzen informed us that snow had been very heavy this winter, & that two days previously a new fall had made the steep upper slopes dangerously slippery — we were a month earlier than the usual mountain opening.

Saturday 22nd was a cloudy day, but we proceeded up the mountain with easy going over the snow & stones to a small waterfall at the lower left base of the arêtes leading to the summits (2 1/2 hrs. after starting). After this the snow became exceedingly difficult so far as the lower limit of the ridge which is the usual ascent during the summers. The guide however informed us that the combined danger of slippery rocks & snow made the winter ascent up the long snow-covered water-course directly in front. This we tackled for some distance, but ordinary walking boots sunk us knee-deep in the soft snow, & the lowering clouds & rain decided us to retrace our steps.

★ The next day it rained incessantly, but Monday showing promise of fine weather S. made another attempt. The rain had percolated through the hard winter snow of the lower slopes, making it into miniature crevasses with hard ridges, over which the going was no more difficult than on the earlier attempt. On reaching our previous returning point we found however the snow to be in a soft slippery state. Donning Japanese snow-shoes, we slowly ascended the increasingly steep snow slope, all traces of rock & watercourse being obliterated by the snow.

For two hours & a half, we scrambled practically on all fours up this

クライマーズ・ブック対訳

1915.5

1915年5月　穂高山(ホダカヤマ)

　5月21日金曜日、徳本峠を越える。最後の1里（約4km）は深い雪で覆われていた。その日は快晴で、峠の頂上からは穂高山の雄大な景色が見えた。上高地・白骨経由で島々まで戻るつもりだったが、あの山の姿を見て、穂高山を登ることにした。

　上高地温泉で、今年の冬は豪雪だったと聞かされた。そのうえ、2日前にもまた雪が降り、上の方の険しい斜面が危険なほど滑りやすくなっているという。われわれは例年の山開きよりも1カ月早く山に入ったのだ。

　22日の土曜日は曇っていたが、雪や岩を越えながら、山頂に続くやせ尾根の左手ふもとにある小さな滝までは難なく進んだ（出発から2時間半）。その先のやせ尾根の鞍部にかけては、雪が行く手を阻んだ。夏の時期ならば、このやせ尾根のルートで登るところだ。しかしながら、岩が滑りやすいうえに雪もあるので、冬山の場合は真正面にある、雪に覆われた長い川を上ることになると案内人に言われた。そこで、しばらく前進してはみたのだが、ごく普通の登山靴を履いていたため、柔らかい雪に膝まで足をとられてしまった。そのうえ、低く垂れこめた雲から雨も降ってきたので、引き返すことにした。①

★　翌日、雨が絶え間なく降ったが、月曜日には天気が好転するというので、S(ショー)はもう一度登ることにした。山の下の方の斜面には固まった冬の雪に雨が染み込み、固い隆起部のあるミニクレバス状になっていたが、前日同様、越えるのは難しくない。ただ、前回引き戻した場所までたどり着くと、雪が柔らかく滑りやすくなっていた。一行はかんじきを履いて、険しさが増す雪の斜面をゆっくりと登った。岩と川は雪

①このパーティーは1915年、残雪期の5月、岳沢から南穂高を目指して登っていたが、滑落者が出るなど厳しい状況で、引き返した。当時は前穂高を南穂高、奥穂高を岳川岳と呼んでいた。前穂、南穂の使いわけに混乱？

slope, having the greatest difficulty in keeping our footing, & about 50 yds. from the top one of the party, missing a firm grasp, instantly started to glissade at an increasing pace downward. A perpendicular snow wall of about 20 ft. in height traversed the slope about halfway down, & it looked as if he were going to shoot over it at great speed on to the lower section. Fortunately as he commenced to pivot from the upright position, his heel managed to drive into the snow, & instantly ramming his other foot downwards he brought himself up, after shooting down for about 200 yds., the water bottle being thrown out of its leather guards far down the gully. Scrambling up again we all three (S., the hunter & carrying coolie) reached the main ridge of the summit & started to climb over the pinnacles towards Minami Hodaka. With the exception of the actual summits however, the rocks were obliterated by dangerously deep and steep snow slopes, falling almost sheer to the Adzusagawa on the one-side, & down the rock ramparts on the other. A strong north wind was blowing & necessarily steadying steps from the narrow rocky section on to the snow-slopes brought us dangerously near falls into the valleys far below. For these reasons we were forced to return. The steep snow-covered watercourse had to be negotiated with the greatest care. Reluctant to leave without climbing the highest summit excepting Takegawadake, we were consoled by the fact that no one, not even the hunters, had climbed so far, so early in the year. Halfway down the watercourse, a similar snow-covered gully branched upwards to the right in the direction of Mae-Hodaka & it is probable that if we had taken this, instead of aiming for Minami-Hodaka, we should have reached the former pinnacle in about the same time as we took for the main summit ridge. The guide questioned however whether the heavy, soft new snow on the topmost slopes would not have prevented us.

♥   The view was magnificent. On the summit knolls the rain & sun had congealed the snow into glistening frozen masses, over which the further peaks of Hakusan & its neighbours could be seen in the deep blue haze, while southward Ontake, Komagatake & Yatsugatake were similarly in view.

クライマーズ・ブック対訳

に覆われ、どこにあるのかも分からなくなっている。

　２時間半をかけ、ほとんど四つんばいの状態でこの斜面をよじ登った。足場の確保もままならない。山頂まで約45ｍの地点でパーティーの１人が支えをつかみ損ね、あっという間に加速しながら滑り落ちていった。斜面の中ほどには、高さが６ｍもあろうかという雪壁がそり立っていたのだが、あまりのスピードに、その雪壁も飛び越えて、さらに下まで落ちるのではないかと思われた。滑り落ちたのは足からだったが、その状態で体の向きをうつぶせにしようとしたとき、幸運にも片方のかかとを何とか雪に突き立てることができて、即座にもう片方の足を蹴り上げて体を起こした。滑落したのは180ｍほど。水筒は革製のプロテクターから投げ出されて、ガリーの底深くに消えていった。登攀を再開したわれわれ３人（ショー、猟師、荷運びの人夫）は、山の主尾根にたどり着き、南穂高に向かって峰を越えながら登り始めた。しかし、山頂以外はどの岩肌も、危険なほど勾配の急な険しい雪の斜面へと姿を変えていた①。片側の斜面は山頂からほぼ垂直に梓川まで落ちており、反対側は屹立（きつりつ）した岩壁である。強い北風が吹きつけていた。ごつごつした狭い峰から雪の斜面に移動するには慎重に足を踏み出さなければならず、危うく何度もはるか下の深い谷底まで落ちそうになった。そうなると、もう引き返さざるを得ない。細心の注意を払い、雪をかぶった急勾配の沢を進まなければならなかった。岳川岳の次に高い山の登攀をあきらめてしぶしぶ下山することにしたが、これほど早い時期にここまで登った者は猟師にもいないと聞き、慰められた。沢を中ほどまで下ると、雪をかぶった同じような岩溝が右上側、前穂高方面に伸びていた。南穂高を目指さずにその道を選んでいれば、主尾根に挑んでいた時刻には前穂高の山頂にたどり着いていたかもしれない①。とはいえ、案内人は、前穂高でも頂上の斜面には深くて柔らかい新雪が積もっているはずなので、果たして登頂できただろう

①前ページ参照。

Nearer, the magnificent collective spires of Hodaka's pinnacles crowned in white snow, glistering in the spring sunshine, added one still further glorious memory of this splendid mountain.

N.B. We all three suffered severely from snow-blindness on our return; we had no protective glasses which are very necessary; also well-fitting snow-shoes, (the Jap kind will do) until the main ridge is reached, when rock-work alternates with smaller snow-slopes to summit. Climbing the snow in upper reaches of water-course is very arduous work & plenty of time should be held in reserve. Thence to summit of Minami-Hodaka under prevailing conditions hunter estimated at 2 to 2 1/2 hours.

Most important that legs & arms are entirely covered — no bare knees — otherwise constant sinking into deep snow & action of sun causes extreme sunburn.

P.S. We seem to have seen Hodaka on the last day of mountain winter, for since Monday (we have been detained at Kamikochi for two days on account of snow blindness) the upper peaks have been rapidly losing their white covering, the trees, which until now have been bare, are suddenly bursting into leafy green, & the whole valley is awake to the coming of the Spring.

A.M. Shaw
P.I. Richard
26. 5. 15

Kamonji has arrived for his bath & tells us that a few years ago two Japanese reached Minami-Hodaka in May, but that there was much less snow then than this winter and he confirms that with the strong wind blowing there was nothing for it but to return.

かと疑問を呈した。
- ♥　景色はすばらしかった。山頂では、雨と太陽で、雪が光り輝く氷の塊に変わっていた。はるかかなたにある白山やその周辺の山々が深く青いかすみに包まれている。南にも同じように御嶽や駒ヶ岳や八ヶ岳が見えた。近くに目をやると、穂高の山々の雄大な尖峰が白い雪をかぶり、春の日の光を浴びてきらきらと輝いていた。このすばらしい山の記憶が、また一つ美しくて荘厳な思い出に加わった。

注意：帰り道では、あまりにも雪がまぶしくて3人とも目がつぶれた。必需品の保護用眼鏡を持っていなかったからだ。ぴったり合ったスノーシューも必要で（日本式でもかまわない）、特に、主尾根にたどり着いてから、山頂に続く岩場が目につき雪面がまばらになるまでは不可欠だ。雪に埋もれた川の上流を登るのはとても骨が折れる。だからこそ、時間は十分に余裕をもつべきだ。猟師の見立てによると、そこから南穂高の頂まで通常2時間から2時間半かかる。
　何よりも重要なのは手脚をすっぽり覆うことだ——決して膝を露出してはいけない——さもなければ、深雪でぬれた状態で日差しにさらされ、日焼けがひどくなる。

追記：われわれが穂高を登ったのは冬山の最終日だったようだ。というのも、月曜日になると（雪目で2日間、上高地に滞在することになった）、頂から白い雪があっという間に消え、それまですっかり葉を落としていた樹木が突然芽吹きだして、谷全体が春の訪れに目覚めたからだ。

A・M・ショー
P・I・リチャード
1915年5月15日

Ridge between Hodaka and Yari, Aug. 1909

The following account is being written in June 1915, from memory. A more accurate account, written at the time, will be found in the <u>Japan Weekly Mail</u> some time in Sept. 1909.

In conversation with the well known guide, Kayokichi Kamijo, on the second evening after my arrival, I learned that a party of Japanese students was planning to climb Hodaka the next day, and that one of the group, a school-teacher who had taken to mountaineering for his health, was planning to attempt to make the passage of the sharp ridge between Hodaka and Yarigatake. According to Kamonji this ridge had never been crossed by any European, and even hunters and the Government surveyors had never succeeded in scaling it all. Having already ascended Yari twice I was eager to attempt this novel climb and Kayokichi readily promised to get the school teacher's permission for me to go.

★ We started at 6:30 a.m. and reached the summit of Mae Hodaka by the usual route at 11:30. After an hour's rest for luncheon we started along the ridge and reached Oku Hodaka about 3. The view on both side was awe-inspiring, especially down the almost precipitous cliffs on our right (N.) to the perpetual snow fields of Kara Tani (Desolation Valley), some 2,000 feet

クライマーズ・ブック対訳

　嘉門次が湯を浴びに来て、何年か前の5月に2人の日本人[②]が南穂高を登攀したと教えてくれる。ただ、そのときは今年の冬よりもはるかに雪が少なかったという。それに今回のように風が吹きすさんでいては、引き返すしか手だてはなかったと、嘉門次は語気を強めた。

②嘉門次が「何年か前の5月に2人の日本人が南穂高に登った」と教えたというが、該当者を想定できない。

1915.6

穂高(ホダカ)・槍の尾根　1909年8月

　ここに記す内容は、記憶を頼りに1915年6月に執筆したものである。当時書かれたより正確な記録は、1909年9月に発行された「ジャパン・ウイークリー・メール」のいずれかに収録されている。

　到着して2日目の晩、あの有名な山の案内人、上條嘉代吉から話を聞き、日本人学生のパーティーが穂高(ホダカ)登攀を翌日計画していることを知る。そのパーティーには、健康を維持するために山に登るようになった教師[①]がいて、穂高と槍ヶ岳の険しい尾根に挑戦する予定だという。嘉門次の話によれば、その尾根はこれまで欧州人どころか猟師も誰一人として歩いたことがなく、国の測量部員でさえ登攀に一度も成功していないらしい。私はこれまで槍を2度登っているので、この新しいルートにチャレンジしたくなった。私も同行できるよう、嘉代吉がその教師に話をつけると約束してくれた。

★　朝6時半に出発。通常のルートをたどり、前穂高の山頂には11時半[②]に到着した。昼の休憩を1時間とってから尾根に沿って縦走を始め、奥穂高に着いたのは3時頃。山の両側は息をのむような景色で、特に、右手（北側）の壁のように切

①健康維持に山に登る教師……以下嘉門次の話というのは、1909年8月に鵜殿らが穂高→槍を縦走する以前の状況を伝える。

②通常のルートをたどり、前穂高11時30とあるが、「山岳」5年―1にある鵜殿の記録では嘉門次の案内で、5人パーティーが宮川から瓢箪池経由で先に登頂し、測量の櫓にのぼり昼食をしていたところへ、嘉代吉（嘉門次の長男）の案内でフィッシャーが南口（岳沢経由）で登ってきた、とある。以後、下山組と別れ、鵜殿、フィッシャーは合流して嘉門次親子とともに縦走。

33

below.

The clouds were getting thicker and lower but we got a partial view from Oku Hodaka. It was evidently three or four hundred feet higher than Mae Hodaka. To the S.W. about an hour's climb away, rose another of the jagged peaks collectively known as Oku Hodaka but which might better be distinguished as Nishi Hodaka. (Nishi Hodaka, by the way, is readily accessible by climbing the comparatively gradual ravine leading to the lowest gap in the western rim of Hodaka amphitheatre. With Mr. J.M. Davis I climbed as far as the gap on June 15, 1915, but rain made it useless to continue to the summit of Nishi Hodaka).

♥ We had hardly left the ruined tripod on the summit of Oku Hodaka when it began to rain steadily. The wind rose slightly. The rocks became slippery but fortunately that section of the ridge is comparatively broad and easy, so with care no one slipped — all wore waraji.

As the storm continued it began to look bad, but even if we turned back we could hardly get back to shelter before dark. Besides our guides were Kamonji & Kayokichi, both of them intimately acquainted with the whole region, in fact, unequalled for just such an emergency.

We continued clambering down the farther (W.) side of Oku Hodaka, Kamonji in the lead, looking sharp in the thickening cloud for the turn-off to the ridge leading at right angles northerly to Kita Hodaka. It was now 4 o'clock. We could see hardly ten yards in any direction.

Finally, after going down until we were sure we had passed the divide, the clouds broke a few seconds and showed us our bearings. We had gone 200 yards too far. We zigzagged across the treacherous boulder heaps to the gap between Oku & Kita Hodaka where the rock walls of the old Surveyors' hut may still be traced.

♦ It seemed risky to keep on, but we continued over to the first shoulder of Kita Hodaka and then found ourselves blocked by sheer crags with ledges of brittle strata. We dropped stones and got only distant reports. We could not see over 40 feet. It appeared impossible. Kamonji said he had never crossed

クライマーズ・ブック対訳

り立った崖が、約600mも下にある万年雪の涸谷(カラタニ)(「荒涼とした谷」の意)まで続いている様は圧巻だ。

　雲が次第に厚く低く垂れこめだしたが、奥穂高からはまだいくらか辺りを見渡せた。奥穂高の方が前穂高よりも90から120m高いことが、はっきりと分かる。南西に1時間ほど登ったところに、他にも険しい峰々が見えた。これもまとめて奥穂高と呼ばれているが、おそらく西穂高と呼んだ方が分かりやすいだろう（ちなみに、西穂高は実に登りやすい山で、穂高連峰の西の縁にある最鞍部まで比較的なだらかな峡谷が続いている。1915年6月15日にJ・M・デイヴィス氏とこの峡谷まで登ったのだが、雨が降ったため、西穂高は登頂できなかった）。

♥　奥穂高山頂の朽ちた三脚③をあとにした途端、雨が本格的に降り始めた。風が少し強くなった。岩が滑りやすくなったが、幸いにもそのあたりの尾根は比較的幅があり、歩きやすい。それに、慎重に足を進めたので、足を滑らせる者は1人もいなかった。皆、わらじを履いていた。

　嵐は一向に収まらず、状況がまずくなり始めた。しかし、ここで引き返したとしても、暗くなる前に避難所にたどり着くのはほぼ無理だ。それに、何といっても私たちの案内人は嘉門次と嘉代吉だ。両人ともこの辺りのことは熟知している。こうした緊急事態に彼らほど強い味方はいない。

　私たちは奥穂高の西側斜面をはうように下り続けた。嘉門次を先頭に、厚い雲の中で目を凝らし、北穂高へと北に続く尾根と直角に交わる脇道を探す。時刻は4時。どちらを向いても10m先さえ見えなかった。

　そのまま下山を続け、もう分岐点を通り過ぎてしまったのだと思い始めた頃、ようやくほんの数秒だけ雲が晴れて、自分たちがどこにいるのか分かった。180mほど進み過ぎていた。大きな浮き石がいくつも重なる岩場を、奥穂高と北穂高の間の鞍部まで縫うように進んだ。測量官が利用していた廃

③奥穂高山頂の朽ちた三脚とあるのは、農商務省の山林班が、それ以前に測量した跡。鵜殿は高さ2尺の杭と記す。

the next half mile of ridge and considered it impossible except with ropes and the best weather. So we turned back to the surveyors' hut and then dropped down E. over the boulders into Kara Tani.

Kayokichi sped on far ahead and in a few minutes we heard his triumphant shout. He had discovered a huge boulder at 8000 ft. under which we all found dry shelter, after tossing out a hundred stones of all sizes. Snow water and creeping pine and a hot fire soon made us forget our fears of a night in the cold open.

◆ The silhouette of Mae Hodaka against a clear indigo sky at dawn was wonderful. To the left stretched Beobu Iwa. The day was crystal clear. We regained the main ridge of Kita Hodaka beyond the impassable section and for five hours scrambled, crawled and balanced on the always narrow and often knife-edged ridge. The gorges on the west were particularly grand. Added to the excitement of the climb itself was the ever changing panorama of high peaks and ranges rising on all sides, for we were constantly above 9,000 feet.

At one point we had to cross a crevasse of five feet with a drop of ten feet. My foothold gave way and went roaring down the chimney below, carrying a ton of debris with it. Fortunately I had hold of a rope held by Kamonji and escaped a bad fall.

♣ At noon we reached the low gap at the head of Yoko Ō Tani, between the Hodaka ridge proper and the sloping gravelly peak above and So. of Bozu Goya. Kamonji and I descended Yoko Ō Dani and reached Kami Kochi at 6:30 pm. The only item of special interest in the descent was a snow tunnel below Beobu Iwa where the river had burrowed through beneath a huge snow drift: 100 yds. long and 15 yds. across and 4 yds. high underneath, where we walked. Kayokichi and the teacher climbed Yari & camped at Akasaka Iwagoya.

August 1911, Dr. S.L. Gulick, G.S. Phelps and the writer followed the same route, stopping again at Kara Tani Iwa Goya, but avoiding by a precipitous detour the crevasse above mentioned. In 1915 I learned that two

屋の石垣は、今もそこに残っているはずだ。

♠ それ以上歩き続けるのは危ない様子だったが、北穂高の最初の肩まで進んだ。すると、もろい地層が棚状になった岩壁に行き当たった。いくつか石を落としてみたが、石の音がこだまとなって戻ってくるだけだった。10m先さえ見えない。先に進むのは不可能なようだった。この先800mほどの尾根は嘉門次すら歩いた経験がないと言う。ロープを携帯していて好天でもない限り無理だというのが嘉門次の見解だった。そこで、測量小屋まで戻り、そこから例のガレ場を越えて東側、涸谷へと下山した。

嘉代吉がかなり先まで急いで様子を調べに行った。数分後、嘉代吉の高らかな叫び声が聞こえた。約2,400m地点で巨大な岩を見つけたのだ。巨岩の下にあった石を大小何百個となく放り出し、雨露をしのげる避難所を確保した。雪解け水とハイマツと暖かい炎のおかげで、寒い戸外で過ごす夜の恐ろしさなどすぐに忘れた。

♦ 明け方、晴れ渡った藍色の空に浮かび上がる前穂高のシルエットは見事だった。左手には屏風岩が伸びている。その日は快晴だった。前日通り抜けられなかった場所を越えて、北穂高の主尾根を捉えた。5時間にわたり、よじ登ったり、はったり、バランスを取ったりしながら、ナイフリッジ状の岩稜が続くやせ尾根を伝う。西側の峡谷は特に壮大だった。登攀できたことだけでなく、見渡す限り広がる高い峰や尾根の、常に変わりゆく雄大な姿にも心が躍った。というのも、標高2,700mを超える尾根ばかり歩いていたからだ。

道中、幅1.5m、深さ3mほどのクレバスを渡らなければならなかった。私の足場が崩れ、大きな音を立てながら大量の岩くずとともにチムニーに落ちていった。幸いにも、私は嘉門次がつかんでいた綱につかまっていたので、滑落を免れた。

♣ 正午、横尾谷の頭にある低い鞍部に着いた。厳密な意味で

クライマーズ・ブック対訳

④廃屋の石垣は、現穂高岳山荘のある「白出のコル」に。山林班の露営用の石室跡。

⑤巨岩が屋根のように乗り、その下に細長く6〜7㎡、高さ2mほどの空間が涸沢中間部にあった自然の岩小屋。戦後一時期、夏は常住者もいた。

⑥猟師はカモシカなど獲物の搬送や登攀の補助用に綱を持参していた。材質は定かではないが嘉門次の綱に助けられたとの証言は他にもある。

⑦「正午、横尾谷の頭にある鞍部」とある。苦労して東穂高（現・北穂高）に登ったが、キレットを通過できないので、3時間ほどかけて横尾谷の鞍部まで下降した。ここで知人と約束のあるフィッシャーは下山する。鵜殿と嘉門次は南岳へ登り返し、中岳→槍ヶ岳へと縦走を完成させ、水のある二ノ俣の「落合ノ小屋」で2夜目を迎えた。

or three Japanese parties has also taken the same climb, but that no one had yet conquered that hardest section of Kita Hodaka.

There is no water to be had between Kara Tani Iwa Goya and Yoko Ō Dani, and in August no snow is passed.

Galen M. Fisher
June 17, 1915

Ascent of Hodaka on snow
May 31st, 1915

A party of three, Mr. Isaburo Nagai, the guide Kaokichi and the writer made the earliest recorded ascent of the mountain on the above date, before the break up of the winter's snow.

の穂高の尾根と、坊主小屋の南側上方にある砂利だらけの峰との間に位置する。嘉門次⑧と私は横尾谷を下りて、午後6時半に上高地へ到着した。下山途中で特に目を引いたものといえば、屏風岩の下にあった雪のトンネルくらいだ。大きな雪の吹きだまりがあり、その中を沢が流れていたのだ。長さ90m、幅14mで、私たちが歩いていた所の4mほど下にあった。嘉代吉と先生は槍を登攀し、アカサカ岩小屋でキャンプした。⑧

1911年8月には、ドクターS・L・ギューリックとG・S・フェルプスと筆者で同じルートをたどった。このときも涸谷岩小屋で休んだが、今回は絶壁の迂回路(うかい)を通り、前述のクレバスは避けた。1915年現在の情報では、その後、同じルートをたどった日本人パーティーが2、3あったが、まだ誰も北穂高の最難所を制覇してはいないらしい。

涸谷岩小屋と横尾谷の間には水場がなく、8月に雪は残っていない。

ガレン・M・フィッシャー
1915年6月17日

⑧この段落では「嘉門次」と「嘉代吉」を取り違えている。宿泊地もアカザワの岩小屋でない。

1915.5

雪の穂高(ホダカ)、登攀
1915年5月31日

永井威三郎氏、案内人の嘉代吉(カヨキチ)、筆者、3人のパーティーがこの日、記録に残る最も早い時期の穂高登攀を果たした。冬の雪が解けはじめる前だ。

The start was made from the onsen at six thirty A.M.; the first continuous snow field extending to the lower end of the rock debris in the lower ampitheatre of the mountain, was reached at eight thirty, from which hour until five thirty P.M. the party was constantly upon snow. (An exception to this may be named the crossing of the bare rocky pinnacles of the final arête.) Profiting by the experience of the party making the attempt one week earlier, we were prepared for sunburn and snow glare, using Vaseline freely upon the face and hands and binding a thin black cotton guaze about the eyes, which diffused the light without seriously hindering the sight. By these means, although a brilliant sun shone all day, no inconvenience was experienced from the snow.

★ We reached the head of the ampitheatre at the foot of the precipitous cliffs of the range at 10 o'clock, and here turned abruptly to the right, following up the steep snow slope in the bottom of a huge gorge or ravine that cuts far into the eastern arm of the range. (This proved to be the same route which the previous party had taken.)

The angle of declivity was at first 25', then 30' and rapidly increased to an average of 45 degrees, while on the upper reaches of the gorge it was fully 50 degrees. The snow was rather soft on the surface, which made difficult climbing; we sank six to ten inches in the snow, at each step, except where avalanches in descending had swept the new snow clear and had laid bare the hard old snow. Here it was easier going, but more dangerous.

The two Japanese wore the local "Kanjiki," or snow shoes with wooden spikes protruding three inches; I preferred to trust to a pair of heavy soled mountain boots, laced high about the leg. For two hours and a half we toiled up, step by step, toward the skyline of the arête, finally reaching it without accident, beyond the complete exhaustion of one member of the party. The writer reached the final summit of Mae Hodaka at 1:15 and was rewarded by a remarkably clear view of nearly all the peaks of the Hida-Shinshu range. Yari-ga-take stood out, a dark, clean-cut point in a world of gleaming slopes and ridges.

クライマーズ・ブック対訳

　温泉地を朝6時半に出発した。最初の雪原にたどり着いたのは8時半。その雪原は山の低いくぼ地にあるガレ場の下の方まで伸びている。それから午後5時半までパーティーはずっと雪の上を進んだ（例外と言えるのは、最後のやせ尾根のごつごつした尖峰をトラバースしたとき）。1週間前に同じメンバーで登攀に挑戦したときの経験から、日焼けと雪目の対策は講じた。顔と手にワセリンをたっぷり塗り、黒の薄い綿ガーゼで目の周りを覆う。ガーゼを置けば、視界が極端に遮られることなく光が放散される。こうした手だてのおかげで、終日、日差しが強かったものの、雪で困ることはなかった。

★　尾根の切り立った崖の麓にあるくぼ地の頭に到着したのは10時。そこからすぐ右に曲がり、東奥深くまで切り込んでいる巨大峡谷の底をたどり、険しい雪の斜面を進んだ（先述のパーティーが通ったのと同じルートであることが分かった）。

　下を見ると、勾配は最初25度、それから30度と変化し、その後は急激に平均45度と傾斜がきつくなった。一方、峡谷の上手を見るとたっぷり50度はあった。雪は表面がどちらかというと柔らかく、そのため登山は難しかった。一歩踏み出すたび、雪に15cmから25cm足が沈む。雪崩が通った跡だけ新雪が一掃され、硬い古い雪がむき出しになっていた。とはいえ、歩きやすくなった分、危険は増した。

　日本人2人は、長さ7cm強の木製スパイクが複数ついた日本式スノーシューの「カンジキ」①を履いていた。ソールがしっかりしていて脚まで靴ひもで編み上げるタイプの登山靴の方が頼りになる。やせ尾根の稜線（りょうせん）を目指し、2時間半かけて一歩一歩必死に登った。パーティーのメンバーの1人は精も根も尽き果てていたが、それ以外は事故もなく何とかたどり着いた。1時15分、前穂高の最高峰に到達。そのかいあって、飛騨・信州の山脈にあるほぼすべての峰がはっきりと見えた。特に目立ったのは槍ヶ岳だ。光り輝く斜面や尾根の景

①ツルなどを折り曲げて作った輪カンジキのこと。これで吊り尾根まで登りきるのはかなり厳しかったろう。

♥ The huge ampitheatre, on the northern flank of the range, known as "Kara-dani," was a glorious sight: a mighty bowl of spotless white, still filled with the winter snows. The impression gained from the summit was similar to that from the "Ortler" or the "König Spitze" in the Tyrolese Alps; Alpine through and through & entirely different from that to be had two months later in the season, after the bulk of the snow has disappeared.

A beautiful curling snow cornice, fifteen feet high and many yards in length, leaned out into space from the pinnacle of the mountain, while a much larger formation could be plainly seen upon the peak of "Oku Hodaka", two miles away.

The top was warm and windless, and from all sides came up the peculiar charming roar of sliding masses of snow, dislodged by the hot sun and rushing down the gorges to the ampitheatres below.

At two the descent began, necessarily very slow upon the upper reaches of the mountain, where the surface snow was very treacherous.

♠ We used the rope in the steep descent of the gorge; and but for this precaution one of our party would undoubtedly have been unable to descend without accident. Half way down the gorge, at a point where the angle approached 50 degrees, an avalanche containing many tons of snow poured out of a subsidiary gorge from the snowfield just under the peak of Hodaka into our ravine. Fortunately for our party we were standing, at the time, two or three yards from the central grooved channel of the gorge into which the snow mass crashed and continued to pass down for nearly two minutes. As it was, the wind and snow spray thrown out by the falling mass knocked down two of the party and we all had a very narrow escape from being swept down. A thousand feet below we found the destination of the avalanche. The last six hundred yards of the snow declivity we negotiated by sitting on the snow astride of each others hips and glissading at fine speed, braking with our Alpenstocks, "à la Swisse".

The Onsen was reached without further incident, at seven o'clock.

♦ In conclusion, I wish to strongly recommend the guide "Kaokichi Kamijo",

色が広がるなか、黒い頂が鋭く空を指していた。

♥　山脈の北側山腹には「涸谷」と呼ばれる巨大なくぼ地があり、美しい景色を生み出していた。冬の雪をいまだたたえ、まるで大きな純白のすり鉢ようだ。山頂からの眺めは、チロル地方アルプス山脈の「オルトラー山」や「ケーニッヒ・シュピッツェ山」からのものと似ていた。まさに高山といった趣で、大半の雪が消える2カ月後の様子とは大きく異なる。

　山頂では、高さ4〜5m、長さ数十mはあろうかという雪庇(せっぴ)が美しく弧を描きながらせり出していたが、3kmほど離れた奥穂高の山頂にはさらに大きな雪庇がはっきり見てとれた。

　山頂は暖かく風がない。雪の塊が滑り落ちるときの一種独特な轟(とどろき)があらゆる方向から聞こえてくる。強い太陽の日差しに雪が緩み、下のくぼ地まで渓谷を一気に落ちていった。

　2時に下山を開始。山頂付近は雪の表面がとても不安定だったので、極めてゆっくり進まざるを得なかった。

♠　峡谷の険しい下りではロープを使用した。ロープの用意がなければ、下山時には間違いなくパーティーの誰かが事故に遭っていただろう。峡谷を半分ほど下りたところで、雪崩に遭遇した。勾配が50度近くある場所で、何トンという量の雪が崩れ落ち、穂高の山頂の真下にある雪原の渓谷支流からここの谷へと流れ込んだのだ。幸いにも、そのとき私たちが立っていたのは、谷に続く本流から2〜3m離れたところだった。雪の塊が、すさまじい音を立てながら2分近く渓流に流れ込み続けた。雪崩で発生した風と雪の勢いでパーティーの2人が転倒したが、全員、すんでのところで雪崩に巻き込まれずに済んだ。300mほど下ったところで、私たちは雪崩の先端を見つけた。麓まであと約550mの地点からはグリセードで下った。脚を広げて腰を落とし、登山ストックでブレーキをかけながら、いわゆる「スイス流」に雪の斜面を滑降した。

who accompanied us upon this most interesting excursion. A son of the famous "Kamonji", he is born to the mountains, is unusually resourceful, courteous, mindful of the travellers' wants, wonderfully surefooted and has an intimate acquaintance with this range.

J. Merle Davis
May 31st, 1915

Eruption of Yake ga take
June 6th 1915

This rugged mountain, (8480 ft.), the highest active volcano in Japan, had until 1911, been in a state of quiescence, save for a number of sulphur fumaroles, during a period of two hundred and fifty years.

In the Summer of 1911, the volcano passed through a period of eruption in which the present craters upon the summit were formed and the contour of the mountain top was considerably changed.

On Sunday morning, June 6th, about seven o'clock, I was awakened by a series of earthquakes which grew in violence until 7:25, when a final shock of great severity caused the hotel buildings to groan and sway to a most alarming degree. An instant later with a deep roar and a series of concussions, the volcano burst into violent eruption. A huge column of black smoke shot from the eastern flank of the mountain at a point about one third of the distance from the base to the summit and facing the gorge of the

クライマーズ・ブック対訳

それ以降は問題もなく、上高地の温泉には7時に到着した。

◆ 最後に私としては、山の案内人に、これまでになく興味深い今回の登攀に随行した「上條嘉代吉(カヨキチ)」を強く薦めたい。あの有名な「嘉門次」の息子である彼は、山の申し子で、すばらしく機転が利き、礼儀正しく、こちらの要望をよく聞いてくれる。それに、足元の安定感が抜群であるうえ、この山脈を熟知している。

②嘉代吉の案内人としての力量を認め、強く薦めているが、その4年後の夏、嘉門次小屋脇の明神池で、腐乱死体で発見された。

J・メルル・デイヴィス
1915年5月31日

1915.6

焼岳(ヤケガタケ) の噴火
1915年6月6日

　尖峰を持つこの山（2,585 m）は日本の活火山の最高峰であり、硫黄の噴気孔が数多くあったものの、1911年までの250年間は静穏な状態が続いていた。

　1911年夏、焼岳は活動期に入った。現在山頂部分にあるクレーターはそのとき形成され、山の輪郭が大きく変わった。

　6月6日、日曜日の朝7時頃、地震で目が覚めた。地震は激しさを増しながら断続的に続き、7時25分、最後に激震が走る。宿泊施設が大きくうなり、倒れるのではないかと思うほど激しく揺れた。その直後、地響きと烈震を伴い、大噴火が起きた。巨大な黒い噴煙柱が焼岳の東山腹から立ち上った。場所は麓から頂上に向かい3分の1ほど登ったあたりで、梓川の峡谷に面したところだ。

①焼岳（2,455m）は日本の活火山の最高峰ではない。

②J・M・デイヴィスが1915年6月6日に清水屋に滞在し、以下に伝えたこの焼岳大噴火の体験記は、極めて貴重である。

45

Azusagawa.

★ This cloud, though partly obscured by morning mist, rose to an enormous height and spreading out like a huge umbrella was rapidly driven up the valley by a south westerly breeze. From this cloud, which turned the morning light into the dusk of evening, a heavy fall of ash of a light slate color was precipitated. This continued to fall at intervals for the next ten days and was carried to a distance of seventy miles.

The fall of ashes varied in depth in the Kami Kochi Valley, from a light sprinkling upon the Tokugo Toge, to a quarter of an inch at the Onsen and a depth of three inches at the foot of the volcano and on the opposite range of Kasumi-dake.

The violent roaring of the volcano and detonations of falling rock ceased toward ten o'clock and at two P.M. I walked down the valley as far as the point at which the trail to Yake-yama Toge and Nakao leaves the main route to Shirahone. Here my attention was called to a wide expanse of green water standing in the woods, a veritable lake, stretching from one side of the valley to the other.

♥ It was evident that the river course had been blocked, presumably by a flow from the volcano. Pressing on by the Shirahone route over a path almost impassable from slime, into which a light rain had now transformed the volcanic ash, a walk of one mile disclosed the volcanic dam which had choked the riverbed. Suddenly, the forest path emerged upon a river of mud and boulders which pouring from a deep cleft in the side of the mountain had swept a clean path through the fir forest, a path 400 yards wide and a mile long, and had poured an immense mass of broken forest timber, rocks and volcanic mud into the river.

Boulders as large as a Japanese house were scattered and partly imbedded in this river of mud which was similar in appearance and consistency to mason's mortar. Attempting to wade out to a point from which I could view the crest of the immense dam, I promptly sank to mid-thigh in the sticky mass and after prodding clear to the end of my six foot

★ 噴煙は一部が朝霧でかき消されたものの、その大半は空高く立ち上り、巨大な傘のように広がると、南西の風に乗り、すばやく谷を上っていった。その結果、朝の日差しは夜の帳(とばり)に変わり、淡いスレート色の灰がこれでもかと降り注いだ。火山灰はそれから10日間にわたり断続的に降り続き、約110km先まで達している。

上高地盆地の降灰量は場所によって違う。徳本峠では軽く降っただけだったが、温泉地では数ミリ、火山の麓と霞岳の火山側では7cm以上積もった。

噴火のごう音と降り注ぐ噴石の大爆音は10時頃になるとやみ、私は午後2時に谷を降りて、焼山峠(ヤケヤマトウゲ)と中尾に続く道が白骨への主要ルート③から離れる地点まで足を運んだ。そこで私の目に飛び込んできたのは、森林に広がる緑色の水面だった。谷の端から端まで広がるその様はまさしく湖である。

♥ 川がせき止められていたのは明らかだった。原因はおそらく火山の泥流だろう。小雨で火山灰が泥状に変わり、道はほとんど通れなくなっていたが、そのまま白骨ルートを進む。1.6kmほど歩いたところで、この噴火で川底に土砂が堆積し、流れをせき止めている火山堰(せき)が姿を現した。森には土泥と岩塊の道が突如としてできあがった。これは、山腹の深い割れ目から吐き出された土泥や岩塊が、幅約360m、長さ約1.6kmにもわたり、森のモミの木々をなぎ倒していった跡である。すさまじい量の倒木や岩塊や火山泥が川へ押し流されていた。

日本の民家ほどある巨大な岩があちらこちらに転がり、一部は泥流に埋もれている。泥流は見た目も粘度も、ちょうど石工が作る漆喰(しっくい)のようだ。この巨大な堰(せき)の一番先が見えるところまで行こうと泥流をかき分けてはみたものの、粘り気の強い泥に足を取られ、あっという間に太ももの中ほどまで沈んだ。手に持った棒で周りを突いたところ、長さ約180cmの棒がすっかり隠れても底まで達しなかったので、天然ダムの

③この噴火以前までは、焼岳南東面の下部を横切り、旧中ノ湯方面の山道があった。

pole, without finding bottom, all enthusiasm for this particular line of exploration vanished.

♦   The next morning, however, having built a rude raft I made the first voyage of discovery upon the lake, poling down to the dam and obtaining excellent views of the volcanic action upon the forest and mountain sides as well as of the process by which the lake had been formed. The new lake, which was about one mile in length and which filled the valley bottom from side to side, had been made by a broadside flow of volcanic mud and debris, which filled the narrow gorge down stream for a distance of six hundred yards.

From the tops of great firs just emerging above the water's surface, the depth of this volcanic barrier could not have been less than sixty feet. The river current poured over the top of the barrier and tumbled down the long spillway, at an angle of 12°, in a beautiful cataract.

The action of the explosion and of the mud ash upon the forest in the immediate vicinity of the volcano and, especially, to the East and South, was of tremendous force as well as grotesque in the extreme. A whole mountain side of noble forest had been swept prostrate, the great trees lying like splintered matchwood, partly buried in mud.

♦   The trees over an area fully eight square miles in extent were so heavily loaded with mud on every branch and twig as to be breaking and snapping under the burden. For several days the sound of rending tree trunks and cracking limbs was heard in every direction. Thousands of noble trees that had escaped the first devastating blast were ruined by the silent accumulation of ash rendered sticky by rain. It was a weird sight and experience to pass through miles of forest, every tree of which was dripping and fairly oozing slime, with branches bowing and breaking to the earth with the unusual weight.

Two days of torrential rain, on the 9th and 10th, caused the Azusagawa to rise four feet, the river water submerging the bath house at the Onzen and rising to the threshold of the hotel. The level of the lake was simultaneously

先端まで行ってみたいという冒険心が一気にうせた。

♠　しかし、イカダらしきものを作り、翌朝には1回目の湖の探検に出掛けた。イカダで堰まで進むと、火山活動が森や山腹に残した爪痕が一望でき、堰がどのように形成されたのかも分かった。谷底いっぱいに広がる幅約1.6kmの新しいせき止め湖は、峡谷を走る川下に火山の泥流や土石流が横からどっと流れ込み、約500mにわたり堆積したことで形成された。

　水面からモミの大木の先端が見えていることを考えると、せき止め湖の深さはまず180cmを下回らないだろう。堰を越えた流れは、傾斜12度で長い放水路へと転がり落ちていく。その様はまるで美しい滝のようだ。

　爆発と降灰が噴火口周辺の森林（特に東側と南側）に与えた打撃はとてつもなく大きく、しかも極めて異様な光景を生み出していた。山腹を覆っていた壮麗な森はなぎ倒され、木っ端みじんになった大木は一部が泥に埋まっていた。

♦　木がすっかり泥をかぶった範囲は、優に20km²はあった。泥の重さに耐えかねて、枝という枝がバキバキと折れていた。それから数日の間は、木の幹が引き裂かれ、大きな枝がへし折られる音が四方八方から聞こえてきた。最初の爆風に耐え抜いた何千本もの大木も、雨で粘度が増し音もなく堆積していく土泥に襲われ、無残な姿に変わっていった。どの木からもドロドロしたものが染みだし、したたり落ちている。そのあまりの重さに、枝が地面までしなり、折れていく。そんな光景を目の当たりにしながら何kmも進むのは不気味だった。

　9日、10日の2日間にわたる豪雨により、梓川は水位が約120cm上昇した。上高地温泉の湯屋は水没し、宿の入り口まで川の水面が迫った。同時に、せき止め湖の水位も100cm以上上昇し、宿から800mほどの地点まで逆流した。出水の圧力はすさまじかったが、堰への影響は表面が2、3m削られ

③以後10日間上高地にとどまり、イカダらしきものをつくり、誕生した大正池を調査したり、大雨で池の水位が上昇、清水屋が浸水寸前になったなどの記録は初見ではないか。

raised by several feet and the water backed up to a point within a half mile of the hotel. This immense pressure of flood water, however, had no more effect upon the barrier than to wash out a surface channel some eight feet deep. It is thus apparent that this new feature of the valley is likely to remain, at least in part, for many months.

Kami Kochi Onsen, June 15th, 1915 J. Merle Davis

On Sept. 1st 1915 a party of 6 people, 3 men and 3 women with 2 coolies set out about 9.30 a.m. to climb Mt. Yakedake. As rain had fallen during the night the way was somewhat slippery with mud and frequent stops for rest and refreshment in the way of chocolate, raisins and nut bread and lemons (skin included) were found necessary.

As far as the old path went the path was comparatively easy but after crossing the valley made by last July's eruption we met precipitous and rocky places. The final rocky ascent was very steep but the chief danger was the loose rocks that rolled down from above as we climbed upward. Thanks to the assistance of the gentlemen and coolies we reached the top of the old crater at about 12.30. Ascending westward the sulphur fumes became stronger and again descending towards the 2nd crater we passed a hole where great puffs of smoke came out, one of the men held a lady's bright green <u>silk</u> scarf towards the fumes and it turned a deep wine colour. Another man tried the same thing with his dark green <u>woolen</u> socks but to no effect.

★ Aiming for "Shin Ko" the new crater, we scrambled around inside the second crater by a precipitous and shelving path which in places was hot under one's waraji.

"Shin Ko" was like great columns of roaring smoke coming out of an

クライマーズ・ブック対訳

た程度で済んだ。峡谷の少なくとも一部は、この先何ヵ月も
このままの状態だろうと思われる。

上高地温泉　1915年6月15日　J・メルル・デイヴィス

1915.9

　1915年9月1日、男性3人、女性3人、合計6人の一行
が朝9時半頃、人夫2人とともに焼岳登攀に向け出発した。
夜通しの雨で道がぬかるみ、滑りやすくなっていたため、頻
繁に休憩して、体を休めたり、チョコレート、干しぶどうと
ナッツのパン、レモン（皮ごと）といった行動食を取ったり
する必要があった。
　古い道に関しては、比較的歩きやすかった。ただ、この7
月の噴火①でできた谷を横切ってからは、険しい場所や岩がご
ろごろしている場所が数多くあった。最後の岩場は非常に切
り立っていたが、何よりも危険なのは、登攀中に上から転が
り落ちてくる石だった。男性陣と人夫が助けてくれたおかげ
で、12時半頃には古い噴火口のてっぺんまでたどり着いた。
西方向に登ると硫黄臭が強くなった。そこでまた別の噴火口
に向かって下り、大量の蒸気が噴き出ている穴を通り過ぎ
た。男性陣の1人が女性の明るい緑色をしたシルクのスカー
フをそのガスにかざしたところ、色が深いワインレッドに変
わった。別の男性が自分の深緑色のウールの靴下で同じこと
をやってみたが、何の変化も見られなかった。
★　新しくできた噴火口「新口」を目指して、二つ目のクレー

①筆者は噴火を7月と思い込んでいるらしい。6月の大噴火後、3カ月もたっていない時期の飛騨側からの焼岳登山記である。

enormous crack in a rock and mounting straight up. From here was a good view of the mountains on the other side of the river and the new, very blue, lake formed since July's eruption.

The descent from the new crater back to Kami Kōchi was one continuous plodding through mud, and over rocks and fallen trees till we came to the edge of a very deep rocky valley and along this dizzy way we scrambled clinging onto the tough bamboo grass the only living thing on that mountain of destruction. The trees, those that remained standing, were covered with a gray ashy mud which at first gave one the impression of mid winter but afterwards one could think of nothing but destruction and the valley of death. There was absolutely no path and every step meant a sure foot and a level head before letting go the handful of bamboo we were clinging to. Then using Japanese towels as a ropes and winding the ends around our wrists we were able to keep from separating from one another though it was almost impossible to avoid slipping and sliding.

♥ Finally owing to the strength and patience of the gentlemen and coolies all reached a passable place across the valley and from there to the lake was easy. We reached the lake at about 4.30 and after a much needed drink and bathing of the feet we proceeded through the living woods to the hotel reaching there about 5.20.

The landlord greeted us with "O'medeto" telling us we were the first foreigners to make that descent by that dangerous route.

F. A. Spencer
J. Rita Walter
A. L. Archer
Davidna Strier
L. Cheves McC. Smythe
W. H. Gale

N.B. See note on opposite page.

ターの中をはうように進んだ。道は急勾配で棚状になっており、わらじを履いた足にも熱く感じる場所が何カ所もあった。

　「新口」では、岩に開いた巨大な割れ目からいくつもの噴煙が空高く立ち上っていた。そこからは、川の向こう岸にある山々の雄大な姿や、7月の噴火でできた真っ青な湖が望めた。

　新しい噴火口から上高地に向かい、泥や岩や倒木に手こずりながら、ゆっくりゆっくり下山していった。岩ばかりのとても深い谷間に出てからは、丈夫な笹をつかみながら目がくらくらするような道をはっていく。この破壊しつくされた山で今でも生きているものといえば、その笹だけだった。辛うじて立っている樹木もあるが、火山灰まみれで灰色に染まっている。一瞬、真冬なのかと錯覚しそうな景色だが、見ているうちに、これは破壊以外の何ものでもなく、ここがまさに死の谷であることに気づくだろう。道と呼べるものはなく、しがみついていた笹の葉は足場を固めてからしか離せなかった。また、手拭いをロープ代わりにして両端をそれぞれの手首に巻きつけて、離れ離れになるのは防げたが、それでも滑り落ちないようにするのは難しかった。

♥　男性陣と人夫の強靱(きょうじん)な体力と忍耐力のおかげで、ようやく全員が谷の先の歩きやすい場所までたどり着いた。そこから湖までは問題なかった。湖にたどり着いたのは4時半頃。からからの喉を潤し、足湯につかる。それから樹木が生い茂る森林を通り、5時20分頃、宿屋に到着した。

　宿屋の主人が「おめでとう」と声をかけてくれた。私たちが、あの難関ルートで下山した最初の外国人だという。

F・A・スペンサー
J・リタ・ウォルター
A・L・アーチャー
デイビッドナ・ストリエ

To follow opposite page:

On the following day, Sept 2nd 1915, the writer, accompanied by guide Saito Kaneji, took the same trip leaving the Onsen at 9.15 a.m. and, after climbing fairly steadily with short halts for observation at the most interesting places, returning shortly before 2.00 p.m.

Unfortunately heavy clouds at the summit prevented any careful examination of the old craters, or any extensive view of the surrounding mountains. Lower down, however, there being no clouds the new craters and great mud flow could be viewed without interference. These make a most impressive sight. The sides of the innermost crater rise almost perpendicular to a height of over one hundred feet, resembling the sides of a well, open only in the direction of the river. In this direction there is a succession of low mud craters, but only from the innermost is there any volume of smoke being emitted.

★ Here, low down, is a large opening downwards, six or eight feet in diameter, through which the smoke rushes continuously with a loud roar.

A light rain rendered the path slippery, especially from the new craters to the river over the new mud flow. The writer however wore boots, which proved more satisfactory than the waraji worn by the guide.

クライマーズ・ブック対訳

L・チーヴィス・マック・スマイス
W・H・ゲイル

注：隣のページ※を参照のこと。　　　　　　　　　　　　　　※次の文章。

1915.9

反対のページ※の続き：　　　　　　　　　　　　　　　　　※前の文章。

　翌日の 1915 年 9 月 2 日、筆者は案内人のサイトウカネジを伴い、同じルートをたどった。温泉を朝 9 時 15 分に出発、特におもしろそうな場所では立ち止まりながらも、速いテンポで登攀した。午後 2 時ちょっと前には温泉に戻った。

　残念ながら、山頂には厚い雲がかかり、古い噴火口を観察することができず、周囲に広がる山々の姿も全く見られなかった。しかしながら、下の方は雲が一切なく、新たにできた複数の噴火口やすさまじい泥流をじかに見ることができた。それはこのうえなく印象的な景色だった。最も奥の噴火口の壁はちょうど井戸のようにほとんど垂直で、その高さは 30 m を超え、川側だけ口が開いていた。川の方角には、壁の低い泥の噴火口がいくつも連なっている。ただし、大量の噴煙を吐き出しているのは一番奥の噴火口だけだ。

★　ここ、下の方には直径 2 m 前後の大きな開口部があり、そこから噴煙がごう音を立てながらもうもうと立ち上り続けている。

　小雨で足元が滑りやすくなった。特に、新しい火口の場所から、これまでなかった泥流を越えて川に出るまでの道が滑りやすい。だが、筆者が履いていたブーツは、案内人のわら

Kamikōchi Onsen
Sept 2nd 1915
Victor C. Spencer

Kasadake

Left Kamikochi Onsen at 6.08 a.m. 31st Aug, 1915 — reached the top of Yakeyama toge at 8 a.m. and Nakao at 9.55 a.m. Pitched camp at 2.45 p.m., about 2 hrs. climb from the timber camp on the Sawadagawa. Weather dull & threatening.

Sept 1st 1915 Left camp at 6.40 a.m. Climbed three separate snow slopes one at a very steep angle — then a very steep ravine full of large smooth boulders & rocks. After this an almost perpendicular piece of hillside covered with slippery grass had to be traversed. A little more rock work & we were out on a long grass slope with a very steep finish which landed us on the main ridge. From this point to the summit it is about one ri & took us one hour getting there ab 11.50 a.m. No view on account of mist.

*****   Mausden

じよりも歩きやすかったようだ。

上高地温泉
1915年9月2日
ヴィクター・C・スペンサー

1915.9

<u>笠ヶ岳</u>
(カサダケ)

　1915年8月31日午前6時8分、上高地温泉出発——午前8時には焼山峠(ヤケヤマトウゲ)①の頂、午前9時55分には中尾に到着。午後2時45分、サワダ川にある伐採用の飯場から2時間ほど登ったところでキャンプを張る。どんよりとした、今にも雨が降り出しそうな天気。

　1915年9月1日朝6時40分、キャンプ地を出発。雪の斜面を三つ登る。一つは傾斜が特に急だった。それから、大きく滑らかな石や岩がごろごろある、とても険しい渓谷を通る。その後、滑りやすい草が生えた、ほぼ垂直の急斜面をトラバースしなければならなかった。さらに少し岩場を進むと、草に覆われた長い斜面に出る。その斜面の最後にある非常に険しい登りを制して、主尾根に到着した。そこから山頂までは約1里。1時間かけて11時50分に到着。霧のため視界不良。

*****　モースデン

①前記パーティーの前々日、清水屋から笠ヶ岳への登山に向かった筆者が、同じルートの焼山峠（中尾峠）を越えていた。

The following party spent from July 8 to the 13th at Kamikochi hotel.

They did little climbing, going up Yake-Yama only part way beyond the toge. The fine views well repaid the difficulty of the climb.

★ The party enjoyed Bear Valley, other short walks and the beauty of the scenery within reasonable distance of the hotel.

The day of arrival was a perfect one for the trip over from Shima-Shima. One other day only was free from hard showers or almost continuous rain.

(Mrs. J.D.) F. H.Davis
Ida W. Harrison
Alice E. Cary
Katherine F. Fanning
Estella L. Coe
Guy C. Converse

Notes, Supplementary to "Murray", on the assent of Oku Hodaka
1. The ascent occupies about five hours and the descent about three and a half.
2. Water can only be obtained in the wood which skirts the base of the mountain.
3. Tabi & waraji are strongly recommended in preference to boots, since the

クライマーズ・ブック対訳

1916(?).7

　以下のパーティーが7月8日から13日まで上高地のホテルに滞在した。

　ほとんど登山はせず、焼山(ヤケヤマ)を峠の少し先まで登っただけだ。てこずったが、すばらしい景色を眺められたので報われた。

★　一行は熊谷などを散策①し、宿泊施設周辺の美しい風景を楽しんだ。

　到着した日は島々からの旅にはうってつけの天気だった。激しい雨が降らなかったのはその他に1日だけで、それ以外はほとんど雨が降り続いていた。

F・H・デイヴィス（J・D・デイヴィス夫人）
アイダ・W・ハリソン
アリス・E・ケーリー
キャサリン・F・ファニング
エステラ・L・コー
ガイ・C・コンバース

① Dr.Jerome Dean Davis は新島襄とともに同志社設立に貢献した人物。「熊谷」はどこのことか不明。

1916.8

奥穂高登攀に関する「マレー」の補足メモ
1. 登りは約5時間かかり、下りには3時間半かかった。
2. 水が手に入るのは、山の麓に広がる森林のみ。
3. 登山靴よりも足袋とわらじを強く薦める。というのも、行程の大部分が巨礫と一枚岩(スラブ)だからだ。
4. 登りはマレーが指摘するほど厄介ではない。おそらく一般

climbing is mostly over boulders and granite slabs.
4. The ascent is not nearly so difficult as Murray suggests, and may be attempted by ordinary pedestrians. The actual climbing is no more arduous than on the peak of Yari, except in that it requires more time.

H. Hutchinson
Aug. 4th 1916

1918

On August 18 Rev. W.H. Elwin and Rev. W.H. Murray Walton made the climb from Yarigatake via the ridge to Oku Hodaka and Hodaka. The climb had been done for the first time the year before by Mr. Mori Aritsune, and some friends. The time taken was 13 hrs. 20 minutes. On the first day weather conditions were good, but afterward the mountains were enveloped in mist, while the last part of the climb was in rain.

A full account of the climb with times etc. appears in the Journal of the Japan Alpine Club in 1918.

WHMW
Inserted 19/ 8 / 30

のハイカーでも挑戦できるだろう。登攀自体は槍の峰と比べて難しいということはないが、時間はもっとかかる。

H・ハッチンソン
1916年8月4日

1919.8

1918年

　8月18日、W・H・エルウィン牧師とW・H・マレー・ウォルトン牧師で、槍ヶ岳から尾根伝いに奥穂高(オクホダカ)、穂高を登る。1年前にモリ・アリツネ氏が友人らと初登攀に成功したルートだ①。所要時間は13時間20分。初日の天候は良好だったが、その後、山々は霧に包まれ、登攀の最後は雨模様になった。

　時刻など登攀の詳細に関しては、すべて1918年の日本山岳会年報に記されている。

WHMW
1919年8月30日記

①牧師ら3人が槍→穂高を1918年に縦走したとのことだが、その前年が初縦走というわけではない。モリ・アリツネ氏については不明。

Yari
Aug 2nd, 1919

Left Kamikochi 12:30 pm. this July 31st — camped ab 2:15 at small bridge crossing main stream — after 45 minutes for lunch hiked steadily reaching Hut at 6 p.m.

★ Owing to rain that started late — 10 a.m. next day (Aug 1st) for Yari — reached base of the mountain (or spear point at 12:30 — On account of heavy fog & rains that hurriedly swept over at this time we turned back — reaching hut at 2 p.m. — at 3 p.m. we started our return for Kamikochi, arriving at 7 pm, having walked the entire way in a drizzling rain.

The trip was fine & well enjoyed in spite of the heavy weather.

Thea Converse
Guy Converse
Gail Reitzel
Ray Reitzel

June 17, 1927
Mr. Takeda, Audrey Forfar Shippam & I scrambled up Yake-dake.

I had on a bright green silk scarf and although I held it in a hole until I burned my hand it did not turn color.

クライマーズ・ブック対訳

1919.8

槍
1919年8月2日

　上高地を7月31日12時30分に出発——2時15分頃、川の主流に架かる小さな橋の辺りでキャンプを張る——昼食に45分、それから着実に足を進め、午後6時には小屋①に到着。
★　夜半に降り始めた雨のせいで、翌日（8月1日）は午前10時に槍へ。12時30分、山（つまり尖峰）の基部に到着。この頃になると霧が一段と深く立ち込め、雨も激しさを増していたので、引き返した。午後2時、小屋に到着。午後3時、上高地への帰途に着く。そぼ降る雨の中を歩き続け、午後7時に到着。
　天候は芳しくなかったが、今回の旅はすばらしく、すこぶる楽しめた。

ティア・コンバース
ガイ・コンバース
ゲイル・ライツェル
レイ・ライツェル

①「小屋」は2年前に開業した穂苅三寿雄らの槍沢小屋（ババの平）と思われる。

1927.6

1927年6月17日
　タケダ氏、オードリー・フォーファー・シッパム、私とで焼岳を登攀しました。
　明るい緑のシルクスカーフを持参し、手がやけどするまで穴にかざしましたが、色は変わりませんでした。

63

June 18—

Started for Yari. Went up the Atsusa. Snow slope up to the hut on Yari in good condition. We were a bit late so did not try Yari today (I mean June 18.)

Lots of snow in all huts.

June 19.

Up at 4:30. Climbed Yari to get an appetite for breakfast.

At 8 a.m. left hut with guide Oi Shokichi, and Hayashi to carry food and two extra blankets.

Made entire ridge from Yari to Karasawa hut by 6.30.

There were some snow fields but a great deal of dangerous loose rock.

This is no climb for a beginner although Mr. Takeda has not climbed to any great extent.

He was fine all the way, but badly done up at the end.

The guides <u>dog</u> got away from the coolie who was supposed to take her back from Yari the way we had come, and followed us.

Several times the guide had to help her up places. The fact of a dog making the ridge is nothing against the ridge but a lot for the dog.

The climb must <u>not</u> be tried in icey or stormy weather as it really is a long dangerous climb.

★June 20.

Left hut and climbed Oku Hodaka and crossed ridge to Mai Hodaka, thence to Shimizu-ya, Kamikochi, reaching there a little before four P.M.

This is a nice rock scramble but, I would scarcely call it "a walk for a pedestrian," as there are <u>many</u> places where an inexperienced person could easily lose his life.

In my opinion, the climbing is fine — from an <u>experienced</u> climbers point of view. So far as <u>this book</u> records, we are the first Europeans (whites) to cross the entire ride from Yari to Mai Hodaka.

It is a good sporty climb, but don't attempt it without one good guide;

クライマーズ・ブック対訳

6月18日
　槍に向けて出発。梓川を上流へ。槍の小屋まで雪の斜面は良好。遅れ気味だったので、今日（つまり18日）は槍の穂先まで登りませんでした。
　どの小屋にも雪がたくさん入り込んでいました。

6月19日
　4時半、起床。朝食をおいしく食べるため、槍を登攀。
　午前8時に小屋を出発、案内は大井庄吉（オイショウキチ）で、ハヤシには食糧とともに毛布を余分に2枚運んでもらいました。
　槍から涸沢まで縦走し、涸沢の小屋には6時半までに到着。①
　一部、雪原も見られましたが、今にも崩れそうな岩がたくさんありました。
　この山は初心者向けではありません。とはいえ、タケダ氏も大して登山の経験がありません。
　ずっと調子よかったのですが、最後には疲れ果てていました。
　案内人の犬が人夫から逃げてきました。槍から往路のルートで連れて帰ってもらうはずが、私たちを追ってきてしまったのです。
　案内人が犬を抱えなければならないことが何度かありました。犬が制覇したからといって、この尾根がたやすいというわけではありません。犬がすごいのです。
　この登山は非常に時間がかかり危険なので、氷で滑りやすいときや嵐のときには決して試してはいけません。

①「白出のコル」の穂高岳山荘と思われる。

★6月20日
　小屋を立ち、奥穂高（オクホダカ）を登攀。前穂高まで尾根を縦走し、そこから上高地の清水屋へ。到着したのは午後4時少し前でした。
　快適な岩登りですが、私ならとても「一般のハイカー旅行

65

first class, heavy nailed boots; good weather and some experience. (No water on entire ridge.)

Dr. Cora Johnstone Best
Audrey Forfar Shippam
Genji Takeda

♥We came in over Tokugo Pass and going out via Nakano-yu Pass.
Weather:
Rained hard all day June 16. Cleared and got cold. Fine weather all rest of trip. Cloudy near evening each day. and wind so heavy at night almost impossible to stand up against it.

    Mr. Takeda's boots were nailed with sharp logger's calks. We — (Mrs. Shippam and I) not having our regular climbing boots, had our heavy walking boots nailed at Tokio with climbing (rose) nails and a few edge nails. The boots were not quite heavy soled enough to stand much nailing, but we got along nicely.

C. J. B.

者」向けとは呼びません。というのも、経験のない人なら簡単に命を落としかねない場所が数多くあるからです。

　確かに登山を満喫できます。ただ、それはあくまでも経験豊かな登山者にとって、というのが私の見解です。本書の記録を見る限り、私たちが槍から前穂高まで尾根を完全縦走した最初の欧州人（白人）のようです。

　とても登りがいがありますが、優れた案内人がいなければ、登ろうなどと思ってはいけません。最高級のびょう付き重登山靴、好天、それなりの経験も不可欠です（尾根はどこにも水場がありません）。

ドクター・コーラ・ジョンストン・ベスト
オードリー・フォーファー・シッパム
ゲンジ・タケダ

♥徳本峠を越えて入り、帰りは中の湯峠経由で出ました。
天候：
　6月16日は終日激しい雨。晴れてからは気温が低下。16日以外はずっと好天に恵まれました。毎日夕方が近づくと雲が出て、夜はほとんど立っていられないほど風が強く吹きました。

　タケダ氏のブーツには、伐採で使う滑り止め用の鋭い底びょうが打ってありました。私たち――（シッパム夫人と私）はいつも登攀に使う本格的な登山靴を持ってこなかったので、東京で丈夫なウオーキングブーツの底に登攀用の（花頭）くぎと、縁にも何本かくぎを打ってもらいました。くぎをたくさん打てるほど頑丈な底ではなかったのですが、ちょうど良い具合で過ごせました。

C・J・B

② 1927年6月18～20日、大井庄吉らの案内で槍→穂高を縦走した記録だが、槍の肩には穂苅三寿雄の、奥穂高の「白出のコル」には今田重太郎の小屋ができていた。

クライマーズ・ブック対訳

「う〜ん、いい気持ち!」
オードリー・フォーファー・シッパム

Ariyake — Nakabsa — Tsubakuro — Otenjo — Nishidake — Yari — Yarisawa — Kamikochi

16th July — Took 3-guides and walked Ariyake to Nakabusa.

17th July — Start on tramp from Nakabusa. Reached Tsubame Hut 8.30, being 3 hours from Nakabusa. Wonderfully clear weather. Distinct view of Mount Fuji for 40 minute en route. Also wonderfully clear panorama of surrounding mountains.

Went to peak of Tsubakuro and back to hut in 1 1/2 hours. Started for Otenjo. Sun keeps on smiling and superb view of Yari and whole range. Planned to get on to Sesho-koya, beneath Yari peak, but due to the excessive heat and fatigue decided prudently to stop at Nishidake, 4 p.m. This hut is uncomfortable, small, cold, and very bad water accommodation.

18th July — To make up for yesterdays enjoyment, rain pours down from 1 a.m. and rains very hard with accompanying wind up to 8 a.m. Hardly did we know that this rain was to hinder us practically all through for <u>48</u> hours, with little openings of barely one hour in between. Leave Nishidake 8.30 a.m., arrive Sesho-koya at foot of Yari peak at 10 a.m. The road for the last 1/2 hour is very bad. Cannot attempt Yari peak due to weather, but decide the trip would be worthless without reaching the peak. Break the night in the hut, trusting to see glorious sol the next day.

★<u>19th July</u> — Still raining. Fairly "fed-up" with hut life. As it starts to drizzle with good downpours at 20 minutes intervals, brave the inclement weather after being duly informed by the keeper of Sesho-goya that the barometer he had, had been sent down lest it may break, due to the severe weather etc. <u>Barometer-makers please note</u>. Ascend to the very peak of Yari. Some difficult rock climbing, where the hands are more useful than the feet. Trust our medical advisers will soon make successful operations in transferring toes to fingers and vice versa. After Yari, descend the glacier of Yarisawa

クライマーズ・ブック対訳

1927.7

有明―中房―燕―大天井―西岳―槍―槍沢―上高地

　7月16日――案内3人を伴い、有明から中房まで歩く。

　7月17日――中房から徒歩で出発。8時半、燕小屋に到着、中房から3時間経過。快晴。ルートの途中で40分間ほど、富士山の姿をはっきり捉えた。周りを取り囲む山々の大パノラマも見事だ。

　燕に登頂、1時間半で小屋に戻る。大天井に向け出発。太陽が微笑み続け、槍と峰全体の美しい姿が見えた。槍の尖峰の下にある殺生小屋まで進む計画を立てたものの、あまりの暑さと疲労のため、大事を取って、午後4時、西岳で休むことにした。ここの小屋①は居心地が悪く、狭く、寒く、水回りも劣悪。

　7月18日――昨日の楽しさを奪い返すかのように、未明1時から雨が降り始めた。雨は激しく、午前8時までは風も強かった。この雨にその後実質48時間も苦しめられようとは、夢にも思わなかった。途中、何回かやんだものの、1時間として雨があがったことはなかった。午前8時30分に西岳を出発、槍の穂先の基部にある殺生小屋には午前10時に到着。最後の30分は道が非常に悪かった。悪天候で槍登頂にチャレンジできなかったが、穂先にたどり着かなければこの旅は意味がないと判断。翌日にはきっとすばらしい太陽が拝めるはずだと信じ、小屋で夜を明かす。

★　7月19日――まだ雨が降っている。小屋の生活にはもう「飽き飽き」した。殺生小屋のあるじから、小屋には気圧計があるにはあるが、この過酷な天候のせいで壊れるといけないので、山から降ろしたという話をたっぷり聞かされたが（気圧計製造元の諸君、心にとどめておくように）、土砂降りが20分間隔で小降りになり始めたので、荒れ模様に立ち向かう

①喜作新道の現・西岳ヒュッテに泊まったのだが、当時は荷継ぎ小屋で、宿泊用ではなかった。

which is all snow, going extremely difficult and slippery and the rain troubling with its unique whims. Reach Yarisawa-koya 1 1/2 hours from Sesho-koya, and with warm hearts but unwilling legs the long "en route" to Kamikochi. Will we never reach it. Kamikochi, Kamikochi! At last Shimizuya. The proprietors of here are kind in not charging for the rain water brought in. Soaking wet is comparatively tame. Drowned rats! But a bath and a bed makes you soon forget the long continuous tramp of 7 hours. With crapons, better result are certain.

♥20th — Went up Yakega-dake (Volcano). Nothing particularly worth the trouble. Path is very slippery and in fact dangerous. The history propped by surroundings at the base is far better than the climb itself. Kamikochi and surroundings.

With more experience and better weather, let us hope to climb Yari and see Fuji from there.

Leaving to-morrow. The trouble is quadruply rewarded.

Kamikochi Shimizuya-Hotel 20th July, 1927
(Mrs.) E. Wilson   D.R. Dauer
John Wilson   G. Scheulen
G.A. da Silva

P.S. This trip is not made for the sake of time, but for the interest.

ことにする。槍の尖峰を目指して登攀。岩の難所があるが、そのような所では足よりも手が役に立つ。世の医師が近いうちに足と手の指を入れ替える移植手術をやってのけることだろう。槍のあと、雪に覆われた槍沢の氷河を下る。これが非常に厄介で滑りやすく、気まぐれな雨にも苦しめられる。殺生小屋を出てから1時間半で槍沢小屋に到着、心はホッとするも嫌がる足を引きずり、上高地への長い道のりを進む。果たしてたどり着けるのだろうか。上高地、おお、上高地よ！ようやく清水屋に到着。ここの宿の主人たちは親切で、雨水を持ちこんでも割増料金は取らない。それにしても、「ずぶぬれ」などという甘いものではなかった。まさに溺れたドブネズミだ！　とはいえ、風呂と布団があれば、あの長かった7時間の行軍もすぐに忘れられるだろう。アイゼンがあれば、間違いなくもっと良い結果が出せたのだが。

♥　20日――焼岳（火山）に登る。特に骨を折るほどの価値はない。道は非常に滑りやすい、というより危険だ。上高地周辺の麓の村々に伝わる歴史の方が焼岳を登るよりもはるかにおもしろい。上高地と周辺地域。

　もっと経験を積み、天候に恵まれたときに槍に登り、そこから富士を望みたいと思う。

　明日には出発する。大変だったが、その4倍は楽しめた。

上高地―清水屋旅館　1927年7月20日

E・ウィルソン（夫人）　D・R／ダウアー
ジョン・ウィルソン　G・ショイリン
G・A・ダ＝シルヴァ

追記：ちなみに、今回の登山では、速さではなく好奇心を満たすことを重視した。

July 27, 1927

My old friend, Mr. Kato, the custodian of this valuable record, has asked me to make a marginal reference to an early visit to this region which he and I remember very well.

In August, 1903, the writer was returning from a trip over the pass from Toyama when he met Mr. Weston on the train and from him heard the wonders of this mountain play ground.

The writer returned to Karuizawa and recruited a party to spy out the land. It included Dr. Teusler, head of St. Luke's Hospital, Tokyo, Rev. St. George Tucker, principal of St. Paul's College, Tokyo, Galen M. Fisher, of Tokyo, George Gleason of Osaka, and G.S. Phelps, of Kyoto. They secured the services of Kamonji and climbed Hodaka and Yari-ga-take, sleeping under rocks and pine boughs. They bathed in the "onzen" out in the open, because there was no inn here then.

★ The following year a party consisting of Messers George Gleason, Galen M. Fisher, Dr. Sidney Gulick, G.S. Phelps, and one other came over here, climbed Yari-ga-take, Yakedake and Hodaka. Mr. Gleason and one other followed the Ridge from Yari to Hodaka. Later Mr. Tucker followed the Ridge from Hodaka to Kasadake.

These, after Messers Weston, Hamilton, Belcher and Miller, were the "pioneers" who encouraged Kato San to open the "Kami Kochi Onzen."

—G.S. Phelps

クライマーズ・ブック対訳

1927.7

1927年7月27日

　この貴重な記録を保管している旧友の加藤氏から、この地を初めて訪れたときの様子で2人に共通した思い出があれば簡単に書き記してほしいと頼まれた。

　1903年8月、富山から峠越えを終えて戻る途中、筆者は列車でウェストン氏に出会い、この山の魅力について話を聞く。

　筆者は軽井沢に戻ると、山の様子を探るためにメンバーを集めた。主なメンバーは、東京の聖路加病院長ドクター・トイスラー、東京の立教学院総理ジョージ・タッカー主教、東京のガレン・M・フィッシャー、大阪のジョージ・グリーソン、京都のG・S・フェルプス各氏である。嘉門次に案内を依頼し、穂高と槍ヶ岳に登った。夜は岩や松の枝の下で休んだ。水浴びには戸外の「温泉(オンゼン)」を利用した。というのも、当時ここにはまだ宿がなかったからだ。

★　翌年、ジョージ・グリーソン、ガレン・M・フィッシャー、ドクター・シドニー・ギューリック、G・S・フェルプスの各氏と他1名のパーティーでこの地に赴き、槍ヶ岳と焼岳、穂高を登攀した。さらに、グリーソン氏と他1名は槍から穂高の尾根を縦走した。その後、タッカー氏が穂高から笠ヶ岳(カサガダケ)まで縦走している。

　ウェストン、ハミルトン、ベルチャー、ミラーの各氏に加え、こうした面々が「先駆者」となり、加藤サンに「上高地温泉」を開くよう進言したのだ。

　　──G・S・フェルプス

① 1903（明治36）年、フェルプス氏が列車内でのウェストンとの出会いから穂高を知り、在日中の英国人ら5人を集め、嘉門次の案内で穂高と槍に登った──という記録は知られていない。メンバーに1909年、鵜殿とともに奥穂縦走をしたM・フィッシャーの名もある。

②翌年（1904）のメンバーの一部が、槍から穂高を、さらに穂高→笠ヶ岳を縦走したとあるのは、日本側の記録にはない。

July 28, 1927

A party consisting of the misses Mildred Roe, Gertrude Garnsey, Madge Winslow, and Doris Clarke accompanied by Mr. G.S. Phelps walked over the Tokugo Toge from Shimajima on July 26th. On the 27th they climbed Yakedake and on the 28th they made Mae Hodaka where they enjoyed a fine view. They broke no records and made no discoveries but they leave for Shirahone tomorrow enthusiastic over "the Japanese Alps".

Their efficient and faithful guide was Nagadani San.

August 6th 1927

I left Ariake onzen with the guide Nakamura Saiichi for Nakabusa Onzen. We spent from Saturday to Monday in that delightful place & started that day for Tsubakuro, spending that night at the Tsubakuro Hut, & starting next morning for Yarigatake, & had a most beautiful walk there, in perfect weather with views of Fuji & many distant mountains. We went via Otenjo Dake & Akaiwa Dake. We spent that night at the Hut just below the summit of Yarigatake. The walk from Tsubakuro & scramble to summit of Yarigatake took from 6 am to 2.15 p.m. We hoped the next morning to go to Kamikochi, via Otani, the Karuizawa Ridge & all the Hodakas except Mae Hodaka (to Kamikochi) but after a wild night, the weather was much too bad to think of attempting it, so we left the Hut about 6.30 am & descending to the low end route, had a delightful walk by the river to Kamikochi, where we arrived about 2.45 p.m.

Next morning we started at 6 am for Lake Tashiro & at 9.50 went off to

クライマーズ・ブック対訳

1927年7月28日

　パーティーのメンバーは、ミルドレッド・ロー、ガートルード・ガーンジー、マッジ・ウィンスロー、ドリス・クラークの各女史と同行のG・S・フェルプス氏。7月26日、島々(シマジマ)から徳本峠を越えて歩いた。27日には焼岳を登攀、28日には前穂高に登り、前穂高で絶景を楽しんだ。記録を破ることもなく、新しい発見もなかったが、明日は白骨に向けて出発予定、すっかり「日本アルプス」なのである。
　同行した優秀で信頼できる案内人は、ナガダニさんだ。

1927.8

1927年8月6日

　有明温泉(オンゼン)を出発、案内人のナカムラ・サイイチと共に中房温泉に向かう。そのすばらしい土地で土曜日から月曜日までを過ごし、同日、燕に向けて出発。その晩は燕山荘で過ごし、翌朝、槍ヶ岳を目指して出発。これまでになくすばらしい登山で、好天に恵まれ、富士や遠くの山々が数多く見えた。大天井岳と赤岩岳を経由する。その晩は槍ヶ岳山頂直下の小屋で過ごした。午前6時から午後2時15分までかけて燕から歩き、槍ヶ岳山頂を登攀する。翌朝は上高地に向かい、大谷、軽井沢尾根①、前穂高以外の穂高(ホダカ)連峰すべてを（上高地まで）縦走するつもりだった。しかしながら、一晩中暴風雨に見舞われ、翌朝になっても、縦走など考えられないほど天気が荒れたので、午前6時半頃に小屋を出ると、下りは上高地まで川沿いの道を楽しみながら進んだ。到着したのは午後2時45分頃──翌朝6時、田代池に向けて出発、9時50分には焼

①「大谷」「軽井沢尾根」は不明。「軽井沢」は「涸沢」の勘違いか？

Yake Dake & gained the summit in about three hours. Weather was very bad. I found Nakamura an excellent guide.

Lucy E Beattie L.A.C.

9th July 1929

Allow me to add a few lines in the Climbers Book left by my old friend Rev. Walter Weston "for the use of European and American mountaineers."

I didn't know the existence of this book until it came in my sight at the exhibition of the Alpine Association, Matsumoto held at Mitsukoshi, Tokio on the 22nd June 1929. Indeed, it was my great pleasure to read his record and those of other foreign Alpinists from the book.

Since Mr. Weston has left Japan after accomplished the splendid pioneers work amongst the Japanese Alps, the mountaineering effort of Japan has reached to so a flourishing state that Mr. Weston himself has perhaps little dreamed of.

★ His name joined with the name of the pioneer-guide "Kamonji," will be remembered as long as the Japanese Alps shall endure.

I myself, being one of the founders of the Japanese Alpine Club under his valuable advice some twenty three years ago, write this by the name of his old friend, and also as a friend of the late Mr. S. Kato to whome the book was assigned by Mr. Weston.

Usui Kojima

岳に向かった。約3時間で登頂。天候は非常に悪かった。ナカムラは優秀な案内人だと分かった。

ルーシー・E・ビーティ　L・A・C

1929.7

1929年7月9日

　旧友ウォルター・ウェストン師が「欧米の登山家のために」と残したクライマーズ・ブックに、私も少し書き込ませてもらいたい。
　このノートの存在は、1929年6月22日に東京の三越で開催された、松本の山岳協会①の展示会で目にするまで知らなかった。ウェストン氏の記録やその他の海外登山家の記録を実際に読めて、実にうれしい。
　日本アルプスにおける先駆者としてすばらしい業績を残したウェストン氏が日本を去って以降、日本の登山は、ウェストン氏が夢にも思わなかったすばらしいレベルにまで発展を遂げている。
★　彼の名は、山岳案内のパイオニア「嘉門次」の名とともに、日本アルプスが存在する限り皆の記憶にとどまることだろう。
　ウェストン氏の貴重なアドバイスのもと23年も前に日本山岳会を創設した1人でもある私も、旧友として、さらにはウェストン氏から本書を託された故S・加藤氏の友人として、ここに一筆記す。

小島烏水②

①信濃山岳会と思われる。

②小島烏水は1905年に創設された日本山岳会の中心メンバー。岳友の岡野金次郎の手引きでウェストンを知り、山岳会創設をアドバイスされた。

風涼氣爽清
山峻徑界冰
上高地水清
淼淼森內聲
萬物中小人
覺微忘亡性
對永時大經
胡不安其分

上高地　一九三〇年、八月、二十二日
Dr. W. Othmer,
（上海）吳淞 同濟大學

Shimidzuya,
30th, August 1930

I have been asked to make an entry in the book, but do not consider myself a fit and proper person to place my impressions side by side with the Alpine experts accounts of hazardous expeditions which precede my entry. I have wandered through the Japan Alps on three former occasions — for the exercise, the mountain air, and the magnificent scenery — and have always been willing to forgo the excitement of climbing for climbing's sake.

★　For the fourth time, I have managed to work my way to the top of Tokugo-toge and gaze with delight upon the jagged peaks of Hodaka. With

クライマーズ・ブック対訳

1930.8

険しい山道に氷が張る
上高地の清らかな水
森の中に響きわたる水の音
この自然界にあって人の存在は小さく
広大な自然に我を忘れる
まさにこの空間に
冷たい風が吹き渡る澄んだ空
なぜそのままの自分が居られよう

上高地にて、1930年8月22日
呉淞 同済大学(上海)
ドクター・W・オスマー

1930.8

清水屋
1930年8月30日

　この本に一筆書くよう頼まれたものの、これまで書かれてきた山岳専門家の皆さんの危険に満ちた登攀エピソードの横に、自分が感じたことを記すなど、とてもおこがましく感じる。私はこれまで3回、日本アルプスを歩いたが(運動のため、山の空気を吸うため、壮大な風景を見るため)、登山のための登山には酔うまいと、常々心がけてきた。
★　4度目の今回、徳本峠の頂上まで何とか足を進め、穂高(ホダカ)の鋭く尖った峰々を眺めることができてよかった。この壮大な

81

nothing before me which can equal in my eyes the grandeur of the Kamikochi valley, I may proceed leisurely onward — towards Shirahone, to Nakabusa, or — with an effort to the top of Yarigatake. Whichever direction I take, I cannot be disappointed.

R Q Dicker / Capt. I. A.
Shanghai
Kamikochi, Aug 1924
July 1925,
July 1926,
and Aug 1930

<u>Later</u>... But we of the "die-hard" hiking fraternity will be driven up onto the peaks by the encroachment of the motor bus and the unbeautiful electric current factories!

5.Juni 1931
Ariakeonsen — Nakabusaonsen.

Bis Shinanosaka ist (das*) tiefeingefurchte Tal, leider der Elektrizitätskultur gegeben, doch dann herrschen die ungebändigten Elemente. Bald nimmt der Geruch die Schwefelquellen vorher, die in dem anmutig gelegenen Nakabusaonsen zu Bädern verwendet werden.

 Tsubakore läßt auf ein großes Gebiet der japanischen Alpen sehen. Lange, weiche Gratlinien stehen im scharfen Kontrast zu den scharfen Flanken der Bergzüge. Die Gipfel erheben sich wenig über den Grat. Einzig

上高地の峡谷ほどのものにはもう巡り合えないのだから、この先、気楽な気分で白骨や中房に向かうか、はたまたひと踏ん張りして槍ヶ岳山頂まで登るか。たとえこれからどこに向かってもがっかりすることはないだろう。

R・Q・ディッカー／I・A大尉
上海
上高地　1924年8月
1925年7月
1926年7月
1930年8月

追記……とはいえ、バスや、美しさに欠ける発電所の侵攻によって、われわれ「不屈の」登山仲間は峰々に追いやられることになるだろう！①

①長距離送電技術の実用化とともに、川の落差の大きい梓川への発電所建設が1920年頃から次々と上流部へ進み、1928年の霞沢発電所の完成で一段落した。関連機材の輸送路として上高地まで車道が開設された。

1931.8（ドイツ語）

1931年6月5日
有明温泉―中房温泉

　信濃坂①までは深く溝をつけたような谷が続くが、残念ながら、電気文化が垣間見られた。しかし、その先は手つかずの大自然が広がる。少し進むと、硫黄泉の匂いが漂い始める。この硫黄泉は、風光明媚（めいび）な中房温泉の浴場に使われている。
　燕（ツバコレ）は広大な日本アルプスに位置する。長く柔らかい稜線は、険しい山肌とは極めて対照的だ。尾根の先にそびえたつ山頂がわずかに見える。その広大な眺望を遮るのは槍ヶ岳と

①「信濃坂」は安曇野市穂高宮城から中房川渓谷を7kmほどさかのぼった地点。大正期まで奥の中房温泉（1,462m）へは、尾根ひとつ南側の穂高牧地区から大峠（約1,700m）を越え、信濃坂（1,200m）

Yarigataka u. Hodaka unterbrechen die weite Schau. Der Vulkan Asama macht sich durch Rauchfahnen bemerkbar.

★ Der Grat zum (****) nach Nishidake ist zu dieser Jahreszeit durch Begehen der unsicheren Schneeflanken sehr beschwerlich. Der Weg ist in schneefreiem Zustand ein großartiger Höhenweg im Bezug auf leichte Begehung wie die Schau.

Von Nishidake ins Kamikoche Tal sehr steil. Im Tal ist oft Pfadsuchen nötig, da die Wintergewalten sehr zerstörend hier wirken. Das Kamikoche Tal birgt neben dem wilddahinschäumenden Wassers und steilen Waldhalden, ein wundervolles Grün der Lärchen mit prächtigen Blicken auf großartige Alpenbilder. Die Enge und Steilheit läßt keine Siedlung zu. In den wenigen Gasthöfen ist Einfachheit und Bergtalfriede.

Möge das so bleiben.

♥ 6.6.1931 Eine Besteigung des (wachen*) Yake zeigte die Eigenart eines geteilten Kraters, während der eine Teil zischt und dampft, ist im anderen ein See. Die Sicht ist sehr vielfältig. Der Kraterrand ist sehr zerrissen, das Gestein lose.

Willi Kraft
D. Ö. A.V.

July 5, 1931

This is a truly delightful spot to which I hope to return before very long.

J Holbrook Chapman
America Consul
Nagoya

穂高だけである。長くたなびく浅間火山の煙が目を引く。

★ （****）この季節に西岳の尾根に向かうと、不安定な雪山を登らなければならず、非常に厄介だ。雪がなければ、見た通りのなだらかな道なので軽い気持ちで登山が楽しめる。

　西岳から上高地渓谷までは急勾配が続く。厳しい冬が破壊的な爪痕を残すため、道なき道を進まなければならなくなることもよくある。上高地渓谷では、泡立つ激流と険しい山を背景に、カラマツの美しい緑が映える見事なアルプスの光景が見渡せる。この土地の持つかたくなさと険しさが入山者を拒む。わずかにある宿は素朴で、穏やかな渓谷を堪能できる。いつまでもこのままでありますように。

♥　1931年6月6日、焼岳への登頂では、噴火口の両側で対照的な特性が見て取れた。一方はシューシューと音を立てて蒸気（煙）を出しているのに対して、他方は湖が形成されており、多彩な眺望である。噴火口付近は裂け目のように木々がなぎ倒され、岩石は不安定だ。

ヴィリィ・クラフト
ドイツ・オーストリア・アルペン連盟

へ下り、中房川沿いに登った。下流から順次、発電所が建設され、懸崖に中房川車道ができた。中房温泉は上高地への梓川車道ができるまで、槍ケ岳方面への登山の拠点だった。

②西岳の尾根とは「喜作新道」のこと。1922年、中房温泉の百瀬家がスポンサーで、小林喜作が大天井岳中腹から槍ケ岳への東鎌尾根に登山道を拓き、殺生小屋（ひごや）を開設した。

クライマーズ・ブック対訳

1931.7

1931年7月5日

ここは非常にすばらしい場所で、近いうちにまた訪れたい。

米国領事
名古屋
J・ホルブルック・チャップマン

20.August 1931

Nach einer einfachen Lauftour nach dem Yake-dake am 11.VIII und einer ziellosen, aber sehr schweren Übungskletterei am Roppyakudake zusammen mit Herrn Raiko Arima ging ich am ✻✻✻.VIII 6.20 ganz allein nach dem Mae-Hodaka. Der Weg, der auf der Karte eingezeichnet ist, ist allgemein nicht zu verfehlen; an den kurzen Wandstücken und den folgenden steilen Stellen, die man nach etwa 3 Std. erreicht, ist jedoch etwas Vorsicht geboten. – Nach 1 1/2 Std. Rast auf dem Gipfel des Mae-Hodaka brach ich 12.15 auf zum Oku-Hodaka, dem höchsten Gipfel des ganzen Gebietes.

    1.55 war er erreicht und 2.20 kam ich an der Hodakanokoya an. Das Wetter war bis zum Mittag schön, dann setzte Nebel ein, der ein führerloses Alleingehen so sehr erschwerte, daß ich auf sofortige Fortsetzung der Tour verzichten mußte. – So ging ich am Morgen des 15.VIII 6.25 weiter; mein Plan war die Gratüberschreitung zum Yarigatake. Der Weg bietet am Anfang manche anregende Kletterei, vor allem hübsch sind der Abstieg vom Karakiwadake, der Abstieg vom Kita-Hodake und der Anstieg zum Minamidake; die übrigen Teile sind einfache Lauftour. Im allgemeinen aber halte ich gerade wegen dieser Abwechslung die Gratüberschreitung für sehr lohnend; auch die Aussicht nach Osten und Westen fabelhaft schön. Zu verfehlen ist der Weg kaum; auch merkt man sofort am lockeren Gestein, wenn man einmal ein Stück vom richtigen Wege abgekommen ist. Wasser gibt es nicht auf dem Wege bis eine Stunde vor Katanokoya. – Ankunft in Katanokoya 1.55, weiter bei Nebel. Hier traf ich Herrn Arima wieder, der mit einem Führer direkt von Kamikochi hinaufgekommen war.

✱   Als gegen Abend der Nebel etwas verschwand, gingen wir zum Koyari; ich führte die Kletterei selbst und bin vielleicht der erste führerlose Ausländer auf dem interessanten Kletterzacken gewesen. Die etwa 20 m lange Kletterei führt zunächst etwa 4 m etwas links der Südostroute empor,

クライマーズ・ブック対訳

1931.8（ドイツ語）

1931年8月20日

　8月11日、焼岳の単調な登山の後、アリマ・ライコウ氏（男性）とこれといった目的もなく六百岳を登ったところ①、厳しい訓練ができた。その後、私は8月***日の6時20分に1人で前穂高(マエホダカ)へ出発した。登山道は地図に記載されており、まず迷うことはないだろう。3時間ほど進むと、短い壁の先に急所が続く場所に到着する。ここでは慎重さが望まれる。前穂高の頂上で1時間半休憩した後、12時15分に奥穂高に向けて出発した。この山は連峰の中で最も高い山である。

　1時55分に奥穂高に登頂、2時20分には穂高の小屋に到着した。天気は昼まではよく晴れていた。その後、霧が出てきた。この霧は山案内人なしの単独登山にとって非常に厳しく、即座に続行をあきらめざるを得なかった。8月15日、朝6時25分に出発、山を目指す。今回の計画では尾根を越えて槍ヶ岳に向かった。このルートでは、はじめに興奮するような難しい登攀がたくさんあるが、特に美しかったのは涸沢(カラキワ)岳からの下り、北穂高からの下りと南岳への登りだ。それ以外の登山行程は単調だった。こうした変化があるからこそ、縦走登山は大変やりがいがあるのだと思う。また東と西への眺望は途方もなく美しい。この道が間違えられることはまずない。たとえ正しいルートから外れたとしても、岩石がもろいので道を外れたことにすぐ気付くだろう。

　肩の小屋まで1時間の所までは、途中に水はない。肩の小屋へは1時55分に到着。さらに霧が発生。ここでアリマ氏と再会する。彼は山案内人と共に上高地から直接ここまで上へ向かってやって来た。

★　夜になると霧がいくらか消えたので、皆で小槍に向かった②。私は難しい登攀を単独で行った。私は山案内人を伴わず

①今は六百山（六百岳ではない）の呼称。上高地の南側に迫る岩山（2,450m）。一般の登路はない。

②槍ヶ岳を大槍と呼び、その西側の約80mの岩峰が小槍（3,100m）。1922年に信濃山岳会員が初登している。秩父宮も槙有恒らのサポートで1927年に登頂。単独でのフリー登頂は相当の技量者。

dann folgt ein Sprungschritt zur Kante selbst, und nun geht es an ihr, zuletzt wieder etwas links haltend, auf einen Absatz. Ein schmales Band führt von dort in die Südwand hinaus; von seinem Ende steigt man geradeaus oder etwas links haltend zum Gipfel. Nach modernen europäischen Begriffen ist die Kletterei mittelschwer, obwohl sie in Japan als allerschwerste gilt. Das Gestein ist im allgemeinen fest. Herr Arima und zwei Führer steigen am Seile nach; 1 Std. 10 Min. nach Aufbruch von der Hütte hatten alle den Gipfel erreicht.

♥ Am 16. VIII. ging ich mit Herrn Arima und seinem Führer zusammen vom Yarigatake aus den Nordgrat (Kitakamaone) bis zum 3. Gratturm und zurück. Man findet auch hier Kletterspuren, so daß der Weg kaum zu verfehlen ist; alle Umgehungen von Gratzacken wurden in der Westflanke durchgeführt. Die Kletterei ist interessant und abwechslungsreich, das Gestein ist jedoch sehr rauh und brüchig. Wasser gibt es nicht. Zeiten: ab Katanokoya 7.00, an Yari 7.15, ab Yari 7.30, 2.Gratturm 9.30, 3. Gratturm 10.40. Aufbruch zum Rückweg 11.50, an Yari 2.50, ab Yari 3.20, an Katanokoya 3.30.

Am 17.VIII. ging ich mit Herrn Arima und seinem Führer zusammen wieder über den Grat nach Hodakanokoya zurück; ich persönlich halte die Überschreitung in dieser Richtung für schöner, weil man die anregenden Klettereien am Schluß der Tour hat; auch wird man das Überwinden der Kletterstellen im Aufstieg als angenehmer empfinden als im Abstiege, denn Sicherungen sind nur an einer Stelle da (Karakawadake dicht unterm Gipfel ein Drahtseil).

♠ 6.50 verließen wir am 18. VIII. die Hütte und wandten uns nach dem Aufstieg zum Oku-Hodaka von seinem Gipfel aus dem Westgrat zu. Nach dem Abstieg in die erste Scharte führt der Weg über hübsche Kletterstellen etwas opponiert in der Nordflanke weiter und umgeht damit den Steilaufschwung des Grates, auf dessen Höhe der ‚Gendarm' steht, dessen Besteigung über die Südostwand sehr lohnend und interessant ist. Der weitere Abstieg hält sich immer dicht am Westgrat; Umgehungen werden gern in der Nordflanke durchgeführt. Von der tiefsten Scharte führt der Weg

にこの興味深く難しい登攀を制し、山頂までたどり着いた初めての外国人だと思う。登攀を始めてから約20mは、まず南東ルートを左方向に4mほど登った。その後、飛び越えながら断崖の壁のカンテに登る。カンテに沿って進み、岩棚の上に出るまで再びいくらか左側を歩いた。それから幅の狭い岩棚のある南壁に向かう。端までたどり着いてから、そのまま少し左方向に登り、頂上を目指す。近代ヨーロッパの基準では、この登攀は中程度の難しさだが、日本では全ての登攀の中で最も難しいものとされる。この辺りの岩盤はほとんど安定している。アリマ氏と2人の山案内人は、ザイルを使って後から登ってきた。山小屋を出発してから1時間10分、全員が頂上に到達した。

♥ 8月16日、私はアリマ氏と彼の山案内人と一緒に槍ヶ岳から北尾根（北鎌尾根）の三峰まで行き、引き返してきた。ここも踏み跡が分かる。そのため、道を間違うことはほとんどない。尾根は西側にトラバースした。この登攀は興味深く、変化に富んでいる。

しかしながら、岩石はとてもざらざらしており、砕けやすい。水はない。

時間：肩の小屋出発7時、槍に到着7時15分、槍を出発7時30分、二峰9時30分、北尾根の三峰10時40分、帰路への開始11時50分、槍到着2時50分、槍出発3時20分、肩の小屋到3時30分

8月17日、私はアリマ氏と彼の山案内人とともに再び尾根を伝い穂高の小屋へ戻った。個人的にはこの方角の縦走がより美しいと思った。なぜなら、このルートには胸が躍るような難しい登攀が最後にいくつかあるからだ。また難度の高い登攀は、登りのほうが下りよりも制しやすいと感じる。というのも、このルートには安全を確保できる場所が1ヵ所しかないのだ（涸沢岳（カラカワ）の頂上下側にワイヤロープがある）。

♠ 8月18日6時50分に小屋を出て奥穂高を登った後、私た

③このルートは「大キレット」。今では各所にクサリ場が整備され、中級者の通過も多い。当時は、鹿島槍―五竜間の八峰キレットと並び難縦走路だった。

in derselben Richtung weiter zum Nishi-Hodaka; wir jedoch gingen in der mit großen, lockeren Trümmern erfüllten Schlucht nach Süden ab. Je nach dem Schneereichtum kann man eventuell auf steilen Schneefeldern abfahren, was wesentlich zur Erleichterung und Beschleunigung des Abstieges beiträgt; jedoch ist wegen der Steilheit und des fehlenden Auslaufes die Benutzung des Eispickels ratsam. Der Abstieg trifft schließlich mit dem üblichen Wege von Mae-Hodaka nach Kamikochi zusammen. Zeiten: ab Hodaka no Koya 6.50, Gipfel des Gendarms 8.20, Ende des Oku-Hodaka-Westgrats 10.30, Abstieg in die Schlucht 11.30, an Kamikôchi 3.45.

◆ Nach einem Rasttag bestieg ich mit Herrn Arima am 20.VIII. noch den Kasumiedake. Der Aufstieg folgt der großen, von Shimizuya aus deutlich sichtbaren Schlucht; nach etwa 1 Std. verläßt man sie und steigt steil auf einer Pfadspur an der geographisch linken Seite der Schlucht weiter.

Bergsteigerisch bietet der Weg im Vergleich zum Hodaka-Gebiet wenig Interessantes, aber der Blick vom Gipfel ist sehr schön. Dauer des Aufstieges 3 – 3 1/2 Std. Abstieg auf demselben Wege, oder über den Roppyakudake; die Überschreitung ist jedoch wegen der dichten Latschen (Haimatsu) wenig angenehm.

Herrliche Tage bei prachtvollem Wetter waren es, und ich hoffe noch einmal wiederzukommen!

Christian Hupfer
z.Z. Universität Kyoto
Kulturvereinigung der Sektion Dresden
Des Deutschen und Oesterreichischen Alpenvereins

クライマーズ・ブック対訳

ちは頂上から西の稜線(りょうせん)へと方向を変えた。最初の短い鞍部へ出ると、北側面をいくらか引き返して魅力的な難所を越える。「ジャンダルム」と同じ高さの垂直に切り立った断崖を迂回して、南東壁から登頂するのは大変やりがいがあり、楽しい。下山では常に西尾根を伝う。迂回する場合は北側をまわった方が良い。最も深い鞍部の道は西穂高へと続く。しかし、私たちは大きくてグラグラした岩ばかりの山狭を南に下った。雪の量によっては、雪の急斜面を滑り下りることも可能である。そうすれば、下山が楽になり、スピードも上がる。ただし、道が険しいだけでなく、ルートを誤らないためにもアイスピッケルを使用するのが賢明である。下山を続けると、前穂高から上高地のルートでよく使われている登山道に行きあたる。

　時間：穂高の小屋出発6時50分、ジャンダルム（岩峰）の頂上8時20分、奥穂高の西尾根終了10時30分、山狭への下山11時30分、上高地到着3時45分

◆　1日休止し、私はアリマ氏と8月20日にカスミエ岳④に登った。清水屋からはっきりと見える大きな山狭に続く登山道を進む。1時間ほどでルンゼを抜けてから、左側の小道をたどり急勾配をさらに登る。

　この登山ルートは、穂高地帯と比べるとあまりおもしろくない。しかし頂上からの眺望は大変美しい。登りは、3時間から3時間半かかる。下山は同じ道を通るか、六百岳を越える。この山越えは、ハイマツが密生しているため快適とはほど遠い。

　好天に恵まれ、とても楽しめた。また戻ってきたい！

クリスティアン・フプファー
目下京都大学にて
ドイツ・オーストリア・アルペン連盟のドレスデン支部文化連合

④霞沢岳（2,646m）。上高地の南側、六百山に連なる。山頂部に三本槍と呼ばれる岩峰がある。一般登路は徳本峠から。

19. August 1933

Am 14. August verließ ich früh 8.20 Shimizuya, um nach dem Sambonyari aufzusteigen, dem vom Hotel aus sichtbaren & kleinsten Gipfelzacken des Roppyakudake. Der Weg führt zunächst in der dem Hotel gerade gegenüberliegenden großen Schlucht empor und biegt dann nach etwa 1 Stunde nach links in die erste Seitenschlucht ein. Die Steilabbrüche in dieser Schlucht werden meist umgangen; der erste läßt sich direkt ersteigen, wenn nur wenig Wasser herunterkommt. Nach 3/4 Std. teilt sich die Schlucht; man steigt im linken Ast weiter (Steindaube). Nach kurzer Zeit bei der nächsten Gabelung hält man sich rechts (Steindaube; die Richtungen sind im Sinne des Aufstieges angegeben). Man bleibt nun in der etwas breiter werdenden Schlucht bis zum Beginn des plattigen Steilaufschwunges, steigt dann nach links auf die Begrenzungsrippe und dort über brüchiges Gestein, durch Gestrüpp und Latschen steil bis zu den 3 Gipfelzacken.

★ Durch Regen und Nebel wurde die Besteigungsroute sehr schlüpfrig und schmutzig; nach vorhergegangenem Regen ist der Aufstieg wohl nicht zu empfehlen. Der Abstieg führt wohl am besten nach einer Gratüberquerung in östlicher Richtung durch die große anfangs erwähnte Hauptschlucht; wegen Nebels, Regens und den daraus entstehenden Orientierungsschwierigkeiten war ich gezwungen, auf gleichem Wege zurückzukehren; Ab Shimizuya 8.20, an Sambonyari 11h. Abstieg sofort angetreten wegen starken Regens; erste Rast in der ganze Tour in der Hauptschlucht 12.20-12.45. Ankunft in Shimizuya 1.20.

15.August: Besteigung des Oku-Hôdaka über den Westgrat. Mit Herrn Schaefer ab Shimizuya 6.10. Auf dem gewöhnlichen Wege zum Mae-Hôdaka etwa 2 Std. aufwärts, bis man nach links in das breite Tal abbiegen kann, das in die tiefste Scharte zwischen Nishi- und Oku-Hôdaka emporführt. Aufstieg über Geröll ziemlich mühsam; Ankunft in der Schart (Tengu-iwa) 11.50. Von

クライマーズ・ブック対訳

1933.8（ドイツ語）

1933年8月19日

　8月14日、朝8時20分に清水屋を出発して、三本槍に登ったあと、宿からはっきりと見える六百岳の最も小さな頂を目指した。この道は、宿の反対側にある大きな山狭の上方に続く。1時間ほど進むと、左に曲がり、最初の山狭の側面に出る。山崩れの急斜面はほとんど迂回した。もし水が流れていなければ、最初の斜面は上端まで登りつめられる。45分後、山狭が二手に分かれるが、左手をさらに登る（石の目印）。しばらく進むとまた分岐点に出るので、今度は右手に行く（石の目印の方向は、登りから見てのもの）。徐々に道幅が広くなり、滑りやすい岩が重なる急な岩場にでるまで進む。そこから左に向かい岩稜を登る。もろい岩石を越えて、やぶとハイマツを通り抜ける。急登を経た後、第三山頂が突き出ている岩峰の先端まで登る。

①前項の④参照。

★　雨と霧でこの登頂ルートは非常に滑りやすく汚れていた。登山前に雨が降った場合、このルートはあまり推薦できない。下山では、尾根をトラバースしてから、前述の大きく主要な山狭を通って、東の方向へ行くのが最善である。霧と雨のせいで、位置の確認が困難になることから、私は同じ道を戻ることを余儀なくされた。8時20分、清水屋出発。11時には三本槍到着するも、強い雨のため、直ちに下山する。12時20分から12時45分まで、今回の登山で初めての休憩をこの重要な山狭で取る。清水屋到着1時20分。

　8月15日、西尾根を越えて奥穂高を登頂。シェーファー氏と清水屋を6時10分に出発。いつものルートを約2時間進み、前穂高へ。広い谷間が続く道まで登り続けたら、左に曲がる。この広い谷間は西穂高と奥穂高の間にある最も深く短い鞍部で、上に向かって続いている。ガレ場を越えて登る

dort wendet sich der Weg nach Osten und führt ohne wesentliche Abzweigung über den Westgrat des Oku-Hôdaka aufwärts bis zum sog. „Gendarm". Ankunft 1.20. Der Weiterweg bis zum Gipfel des Oku-Hôdaka bietet einige interessante Klettereien; man hält sich für meist in der Nordflanke. 2.50 erreichen wir den Gipfel, und 3.20 lauften wir in Hôdaka no koya an.

♥ 16.August: Besteigung des Mae-Hôdaka über den Nordgrat. Ab Hôdaka no koya 6.10 mit Herrn Dr.Heinze, Schaefer und Träger Okuhara Harutoshi nach Osten in die Schlucht hinunter. Man hält sich nach rechts, um dann im weiten Bogen durch die Kamm die Schlucht zu gewinnen, die in die Scharte unterhalb des dritten großen Steilabsturzes (vom Gipfel aus gezählt) führt. Ankunft in der Scharte 8 h. Der erste der nun folgenden Grataufschwünge ist leicht, der Weg führt meist über bewachsenes, brüchiges Gestein. Am Gipfel dieses ersten Gratturmes 8.45. Der zweite Turm weist einige richtige, interessante Kletterstellen auf; auf seinem Gipfel Rast 9.25-9.45, dann Abstieg in die Scharte vor dem letzten schwierigsten Grat. Aufschwung (9.55), der 10.30 überwunden war. Ankunft auf dem Gipfel des Mae-Hôdaka 10.45; 1 Std. Rast, dann wegen Regens beschleunigter Marsch nach dem Oku-Hôdaka (11.45-12.55) und zur Hütte.

♠ Die Kletterei ist für Geübte nicht schwer; wir gingen ohne Seil, wegen der Brüchigkeit des Gesteins ist jedoch Vorsicht geboten. Ein Steinschlag und das Ausbrechen eines großen, sehr tiefer scheinenden Trittes bei einem der Teilnehmer verliefen glücklicherweise ohne ernsten Unfall.

17.August: Gratüberschreitung zur Katanokoya am Yari, 6.20 -3h. Eiin Versuch, am gleichen Tag noch den Koyari zu besteigen mußte wegen eines Gewitterregens noch in halber Höhe abgebrochen werden.

18.August: früh Besteigung des Ô-yari, dann nach dem Frühstück Aufbruch zum Koyari. An der Ersteigung beteiligten sich die Herrn Schade und Schaefer; wir erreichten den Gipfel 9h und waren 10.15 wieder auf der Hütte. 12h-7.15 Rückmarsch nach Kamikôchi.

のはかなり骨が折れる。11 時 50 分、短い鞍部（天狗岩）に到着。そこから道は東へと続く。奥穂高の西尾根を越えて、いわゆる「ジャンダルム」まで縦走する。目立つ分岐はなかった。1 時 20 分到着。ジャンダルムの先には奥穂高の頂上まで何カ所か、難しいがおもしろい登攀が残っている。ほとんどは北側を縦走する。2 時 50 分に頂上に到着。3 時 20 分に穂高の小屋に到着。

♥　8 月 16 日：北尾根を越えて前穂高へ登る。ドクター・ハインツェとシェーファー氏と荷役人のオクハラ・ハルトシと共に 6 時 10 分に穂高の小屋を出発し、東へ向かい山狭を下る。まずは右に進み、尾根を大きく巻くと山狭にたどり着く。山狭の先には、（頂上から数えて）第三番目の大きな急傾斜の断崖の下に短い鞍部がある。この鞍部へは 8 時に到着。さらに続く切り立った断崖が続くが、最初の壁は容易である。この道の先には、大部分が草で覆われたもろい岩石がある。8 時 45 分、一峰の頂上到着。二峰には、登り甲斐のある難所がいくつかあった。二峰の頂上で 9 時 25 分から 9 時 45 分まで休憩をとる。そこから短い鞍部へ下りる。この先にある岩稜は最後にして最大の難所だ。切り立った断崖の登攀を 9 時 55 分開始、10 時 30 分に登攀終了。10 時 45 分、前穂高の山頂に到着。1 時間の休息後、降雨のため速度を上げて奥穂高に向かう（11 時 45 分から 12 時 55 分）。小屋に到着。

♠　この難しい登攀だが、熟練した人にとっては難しくはない。私たちはロープなしに登ったが、岩石が砕けやすいので慎重さが望まれる。落石があったり、パーティーのうち 1 人の足取りが重くなったりしたが、幸いにも重大な事故は起こらなかった。

　8 月 17 日：6 時 20 分〜3 時、槍にある肩の小屋に向かい、尾根を横断。同日、小槍も登攀しようとしたが、半分まで登ったものの、雷雨のため断念せざるを得なかった。

　8 月 18 日：早朝、大槍に登る。朝食後には小槍へ出発。登

②涸沢の雪渓をつめ、3・4 のコルあたりから前穂高北尾根を縦走し、前穂に登頂した。このパーティーはフリーで登っているので、かなりのベテラン。ドイツ・オーストリア勢の技量の高さをうかがわせる。

③現在、北尾根の岩峰の呼称は、上方より数える。つまり一峰は前穂高のピーク。

Christian Hupfer
Klettervereinigung d. Sektion Dresden des
Deutschen u. Oesterreichischen Alpenvereins

Seit W. Weston, der dem Hidagebirge den Namen „Japanische Alpen" gab, hat auch die Wissenschaft in immer zunehmenderem Maße ihre Aufmerksamkeit auf diese Bergwelt gelenkt. „Alpen" müssen oder müßten Gletscher haben; ihre Spuren zu finden, weilte ich mit meiner Frau in Kamikôchi und durchstreifte mit einem japanischen Studenten und dem Bergführer Kozusan das Gebiet. Die Eiszeitforschung in den jap. Alpen hat schon eine Geschichte; sie beginnt eigentlich 1881, aber erst 1903 ist sie von Yamasaki auf wissenschaftliche Ebene gebracht worden. 1913 waren die deutschen Geographen Alfred Hettner und Heinrich Schmittheuner im Agusagawa-Tal; Hettner fand den bekannten Hettner-Stein oberhalb Shimashima; er stellte endgültig die Behauptung eiszeitlicher Begletscherung auf. Als sein Schüler bin ich nun hier, um diese Frage zu klären. Ich bin in der glücklichen Lage, auf inzwischen erschienenen Arbeiten japanischer Gelehrter aufbauen zu können. Wir bestiegen zu vieren den Okuhodake, Karasawadake, Kitahodake, Minamidake, Nakadake, Okami, und Yarigatake in einer Kammtour, wir stiegen hinein in die einzelnen Kare, durchwanderten die Täler zu beiden Seiten der Kette und setzten die Studien am Ôtakiyama fort. Auch der Yakedake, der eine nicht unwesentliche Rolle in der ganzen Frage spielt,

攀にはシャーデ氏とシェーファー氏も参加。9時、頂上に到着。10時15分、小屋に戻る。12時〜7時15分、上高地へ帰還。

クリスティアン・フプファー
ドイツ・オーストリア・アルペン連盟のドレスデン支部、登攀連合

1934.8（ドイツ語）

飛騨山脈を「日本アルプス」と名付けたW・ウェストン①以来、学者たちがこの山の世界に一層注目するようになった。「日本アルプス」には氷河があるはず、あるいは、あったはずだ。その痕跡を見つけようと、私は妻と上高地に滞在し、日本人学生と山案内人のコウズさんと一緒に、この地域をくまなく捜し回った。日本アルプスの氷河期の調査はすでに歴史がある。調査そのものが始まったのは1881年だが、氷河期調査が日本人の学者山崎により学問的水準に押し上げられたのは1903年のことだ。1913年、ドイツの地理学者のアルフレッド・ヘットナー②とハインリッヒ・シュミットホイナーが梓川の渓谷を訪れた。そのときヘットナーは、島々の上方で有名なヘットナー石を発見した。そこで、彼は氷河期に氷河ができたと結論付け、学説をたてた。彼の教え子である私は、その推論が正しいことを明らかにするために今ここにいる。山崎がその後発表した研究論文を基にして、幸運にもよりどころとなるものができた。私たち4人は奥穂高、涸沢岳、北穂高、南岳、中岳、大喰、槍ヶ岳の尾根を登り、それぞれの山のカールを歩いた。連峰では尾根の両側の谷にも足を運

①ウェストンではなく、W・ガウランド。

②ドイツ地理学界の権威。日本にも氷河が存在したとの推論の調査に1913年来日。松本市安曇明ヶ平の梓川左岸に、擦痕のある巨石を見つけ、推拠とした。が、その後の学界の論争で、石質などから否定された。氷河の存在は、最近の調査で立山や鹿島槍雪渓で実存が認定された。

wurde bestiegen. Dort trafen wir mehrere Europäer, die in dem inzwischen errichteten Imperial Hotel wohnen. Die Alpen werden immer mehr zur Mode werden und künftig wird dieses schöne Buch noch weniger Prozent der hier reisenden Fremden erfassen als bisher. Hoffen wir, dass wenigstens die im Geiste Westons Reisenden in diesem Hause bleiben!

Kamikôchi, 9. August 1934.
Dr. Martin Schwind
Ina Schwind

Approach to Yari-ga-take
Lo, as we climb the glaciered ascent
And toil the twisting trail through leafy wood
So scarce of birds but rich in flowered good,
Where round the spur where cataracts have bent,
The majesty of Yari's pointed spire,
The Matterhorn of Japan's alpine range,
Stares there before us, suddenly and strange,

And lifts its naked steeple ever higher.
There stands the crest that beckons to our feet,
A pointed shaft of rugged brittle stone;
Above all other peaks it stands alone
The sentinel, ambition's goal to meet.

クライマーズ・ブック対訳

び、大滝山で研究を継続した。焼岳にも登っている。この山は、氷河のあらゆる疑問に対して、ある意味重要な役割を果たしている。今回の滞在では、建築されたばかりの帝国ホテルに滞在している多くのヨーロッパ人に出会った。日本アルプスの登山はますます人気が高まるだろうが、今後この地を訪れる外国人登山者でこのすばらしい本に心を動かされる人は、これまでより少なくなるだろう。少なくともウェストンの精神をくむ旅行者はこの宿を離れないことを望む。

上高地、1934年8月9日
ドクター・マーティン・シュヴィント
イナ・シュヴィント

1934.8～9

<u>槍ヶ岳への道</u>
見よ、氷河抱きし斜面を登り
緑濃き森を抜け、曲がりくねる道を進みゆく
鳥の姿なくとも、花は咲き誇り
谷を曲がりて奔流は進みゆく
空を指す、荘厳な槍の穂先
日本の山のマッターホルンよ
こつぜんと現れし、その未知なる姿
尖峰のあらわな岩肌、上へ上へとそそり立つ

われら誘い、そびえる頂き
切り立ちし、もろい岩の穂先となる
連なる峰に、孤高の頂き
歩哨(ほしょう)の高き志を得る

Our eyes have seen, our restless feet aspire
To mount the crest of that high splendid sire.

Ascent of Yari-ga-take
So here at last, the final rock is scaled,
The striving's o'er, the toiling and the pain,
And topmost crest of all the Alps our gain,
We stand supreme upon the peak, regaled
With god-like view of all this Alpine world.
Sun-touched with beauty spread before us here,
Fold upon fold of serrate ridges clear

Got spread before us as a map unfurled.
Stand here, O man, and lift your arms to heaven
In worship, and in spirit offer praise,
For after rain and cloud and storm-bound days
At last we are this rare sublimity given.
We've conquered Yari-dake on this morn
When once again the Alps shine out reborn.

Sessho Hutte, Yari-ga-take
August 29th 1934
K.P. Kirkwood

To Rev. Walter Weston

He came and saw and conquered. Even so
Imperial Caesar from the Appennine
Came o'er the Alps, and marching to the Rhine

視界に捉え、足はとどまること知らず
目指すはその麗しの高き峰なり

槍ヶ岳の登攀
そして今、終の岩を極めるとき
　労（いたず）き、苦しみ、すべての歩みが報われるとき
アルプスの、山々を見下ろす尖峰で
頂の、極みに出で立ち目をやれば
この山岳の、神がごとき眺め広がる
降り注ぐ、陽の光で美しさ増し
　峻嶮（しゅんけん）な山容の線きわやかに

神の御手により広がるは、まさに地図が開かれるごとし
ああ、この頂に立ち、その腕で天を仰ぎ
祈りと賛美に包まれる
雨、雲、嵐に幾日も、すべての自由が奪われて
ついに手にした、稀有（けう）なひととき
この暁のなか、わがものにした槍岳
生まれ変わしアルプスが、今再び輝きを放つ

1934年8月29日
槍ヶ岳　殺生小屋
K・P・カークウッド

ウォルター・ウェストン牧師へ

ウェストンは、来た、見た、勝った。
将軍カエサルのアルプス越えのように。
アペニン山脈からライン川に行軍、

Saw Gaul outspread, and conquering his foes
An empire forged. So too did Hannibal
With Trains of elephants march o'er the range
Of high-flung Alps to fall on Rome. Less strange
Were Weston's marches o'er these mountains tall.
A man of God, he knew how mountains stood
Closer to heav'n, and how the godhead dwelt
On spired peaks; on Yari's crest he knelt
In prayer and praise. His conquerings more good
Than Caesar's sway or Hannibal's vain goal,
Weston has given These Alps an aureole.

Kamikochi, Sept. 2, 1934

Though I didn't climb any Japanese mountains up to the present I ascended many in other countries. Several volcanoes I have "done" and whenever somebody, keen on mountaineering after reading those lines, visit <u>Java</u> & E.T., don't forget to climb the <u>Salak</u>, the <u>Gedek</u>, the <u>Tang koe banprao</u>, or the burning, grumbling "Bromo", which is perhaps the easiest to climb, but the curious surroundings, "the Sandsea", and old crater of enormous measures, and the actual look inside the nowadays crater, a real hell, can never be forgotten!

    Cordial greetings to Alpine climbers of Japan

N. Abbinga
Holland
27 Sept. 1934

広範囲にわたるガリアを目にする。敵に勝利、
帝国は拡大を続ける。それはまた将軍ハンニバルも同じ。
象の部隊を率いてアルプスの高みからローマをも襲う。
翻り、ウェストン登山隊の山越えは奇異にあらず。
聖職者、ウェストンは知っていた。
山は天国により近いことを。
山の尖峰には神が宿ることを。
槍の穂先でひざまずき、山々に祈りと賛美をささげる。
カエサルの支配、ハンニバルのむなしき結末よりも、
価値高きものを極めながら、
ウェストンはこのアルプスの山々に栄冠を授ける。

1934年9月2日　上高地

1934.9

　これまで日本の山は一切登ったことがなかったが、他の国ではいくつも登ってきた。火山もいくつか「制覇」している。この記録を読んで登山に関心を持ち、ジャワ島と東ティモールを訪ねる機会のある人は、必ずサラク山やグデ山①、タンクバンプラフ山、ごう音をたてる活火山の「ブロモ山」に登るように。一番登りやすいのはおそらくこのブロモ山だ。興味深い地形の数々、「砂海」、巨大な旧火口、それに、地獄さながらの現在の火口は、一度見たら決して忘れられないだろう！
　日本の登山家の皆さんへ。

1934年9月27日
N・アブビンガ
オランダ

①「the Gedek」はthe Gedek Gn Gededato（グデ山）、また「Tangkoe banpraó」はTangkuban Perahu（タンクバンプラフ山）と推測される。

Bericht über Kletterfahrten
im Hodaka-Gebiet
im August 1934

I. "Gendarm" im Westgrat des Okuhodaka.
Der Gendarm zieht im Grat nach NW, dessen einzelne Türme in der japanischen Literatur vom Gipfel aus zählend als I., II., III., übs. als Terrasse bezeichnet werden.

1.) Eine hübsche, kleine Kletterei ist die Ersteigung des Gendarms über diesen Grat von der V. Terrasse aus; der Einstieg wird erreicht, indem man entweder die erste Schuttrinne nördlich vom Gipfel des Okuhodaka nach Westen hinabsteigt, oder indem man vom Gipfel des Okuhodaka aus dem Westgrat folgend bis in eine tiefe Scharte absteigt (aus der der Weiterweg leicht rechts haltend auf schmalen Bändern durch eine Steilwand führt). Von dieser Scharte aus geht es nun nach rechts (NW) hinab. Bald sieht man links die etwa 150 m hohen Steilabstürze des Gendarms und der ersten Terrasse; unter ihnen geht es wieder ein Stück leicht aufwärts zu einer kleinen Scharte und weiter in derselben Richtung die folgende Rinne hinab, von der aus man vielen Stellen den links davon aufsteigenden NW-Grat des Gendarms erreichen kann. Am Grat hält man sich, möglichst links an der Kante; bei Schwierigkeiten kann man nach rechts in bewachsene Schrofen ausweichen.

2.) Nordwand des Gendarms (1.Begehung (?) 20. VIII. 34) : Die Nordwände des Hauptgipfels und der ersten Terrasse sind getrennt durch eine breite Schlucht; in ihr geht es links haltend hinauf zu einem Kamm, der auf einem Vorbau der Nordwand des Hauptgipfels führt. Den hier in der glatten Wand emporziehenden Riß hinauf (einige gute Griffe!) zu leichtem, geneigtem Gelände, über das man an die Schlußwand gelangt. Durch Spalten leicht

クライマーズ・ブック対訳

1934.8（ドイツ語）

難しい登攀ルートに関する報告
穂高地帯にて
1934年8月

Ⅰ．奥穂高の西尾根にある「ジャンダルム」

　このジャンダルム①は西尾根にあり、北西に延びている。日本の文献によると、それぞれの岩塔はジャンダルムの頂上から見て、第1、第2、第3と数えて、第○テラスと名付けられている。

1) 第5テラスからジャンダルムまでの西尾根縦走は、距離は短いものの、難度が高く、登りがいがある。壁の取り付きは、奥穂高の頂上の北側にある最初の岩屑のリンネを西に下りる、もしくは、奥穂高の頂上から西尾根をたどり、深く短い鞍部まで下りるとよい（この鞍部からはやや右側に向かい、狭い岩棚を険しい壁沿いに進む）。短い鞍部を過ぎたら、右手（北西）に巻く。間もなく左手に、高さ約150ｍのジャンダルムと第1テラスの険しい断崖が見える。断崖の下には再びゆるやかな区間があり、小さな短い鞍部まで登る。引き続き同じ方向に進み、リンネを下る。リンネの左手を登るとジャンダルムの北西側の尾根に出る。尾根ではカンテに接してできる限り左側を進む。それが困難な場合には、草付きの非常に険しい岩壁の方へ右側にトラバースすることも可能。

2) ジャンダルムの北壁（第1登山（？）1934年8月20日）
　主峰頂上の北壁と第1テラスの北壁は、幅の広い山狭で隔てられている。リンネは左側を稜線まで登る。この稜線は主峰頂上の北壁突出部分に続いている。突出部にたどり着いたら、滑りやすい壁に走る割れ目を伝いながら（格好のグリッ

①岩山の穂高岳や剣岳には、「ロバの耳」とか「クレオパトラニードル」だの、特異な岩峰名がある。そのひとつ「ジャンダルム」は、奥穂高の「護衛峰」の意味。いずれも昭和に入って学生登山者らが勝手に命名した。

rechts haltend zum Gipfel; Ausstieg wenige Meter rechts vom höchsten Punkt. Mittelschwer, stellenweise sehr brüchig.

3.) Nordwand der ersten Terrasse (1.Begehung 14. VIII 34): Wenige Meter rechts der Schlucht zwischen Hauptgipfel und der ersten Terrasse gerade hinauf durch eine Folge von Rinnen und Rissen bis zu einem breiten, schuttbedeckten Band in etwa 2/3 Höhe der Wand. Von hier weiter an der Schlußwand empor bis zum unteren der zwei auffallenden gelben Flecken; Quergang nach rechts bis zum Einstieg in eine Rinne. In ihr, einen Überhang rechts umgehend, hinauf zum Grat und weiter leicht zum Gipfel. Die Kletterei ist schwer, das Gestein zum Teil sehr brüchig. Zeit: Vom Einstieg 1 1/2 Std.

II. Maehodaka- Nordostwand (2.Beg. 16. VIII. 34)
Vor der Scharte vor dem letzten Steilaufschwung des Maehodaka-Nordgrates nach Osten etwa 80 m in einer Schlucht absteigend; heikler Quergang nach rechts über (S) über bewachsenes Gelände bis zum Einstieg in die eigentliche Steilwand. In ihr zunächst auf einem Bande, danach durch flache Rinnen schräg links aufwärts bis zu einer großen Terrasse. Bis hierher mittelschwer, aber sehr brüchig. Die Wand wird nun steiler, und das Gestein sieht heller aus. Auf der Terrasse nach rechts bis zum Ende (rechts ist ein kleines Türmchen sichtbar). Von hier schräg nach links aufwärts bis zu einem kurzen Kamin; durch ihn empor und zu leichterem Gelände und ohne Schwierigkeiten zum Gipfel. Im zweiten Teil schwer und brüchig. Zeit: Vom Einstieg 3 1/2 Std.

III. Byobu-Iwa-Nordostweg (I.Rinne) (1.direkte Durchsteigung 17.VIII 34)
Der Weg führt im allgemeinen in der östlich des großen Mittelpfeilers gelegenen Rinne empor. Den Einstieg erreicht man am besten, indem man in der Gegend des Yokoodani-Iwagoya den Bach durchwatet; auf dem Südufer geht es dann in etw. 1 Std. durch eine Geröllrinne zum Einstieg. Die ersten etwa 100 m dicht links neben der tiefsten Wasserrinne über glattgeschliffene

プがいくつかある）、傾斜が緩い場所まで登る。これを越えると最終壁に到達する。長い割れ目を通り、やや右側を頂上に向かって進む。下山は最も高い地点から数メートル右へ行く。中ぐらいの難しさ。所々非常に崩れやすい場所がある。

3）第1テラスの北壁（1934年8月14日、第1登山）
　主峰頂上と第1テラスの間の山狭を右方向に数メートル登る。リンネや割れ目が続いたあと、壁の約3分の2の高さにある、岩屑で覆われた広い岩棚まで登る。そこからさらに最終壁を登攀し、二つある黄色い目印の下まで進む。斜登降でリンネを右手に進んだら、壁に取り付く。リンネでは、オーバーハングを右へ迂回する。尾根までたどり着けば、登頂は容易だ。このルートは骨が折れる。岩石がとても壊れやすい箇所がある。時間：取り付きから1時間半

Ⅱ．前穂高―北東壁（第2登山・1934年8月16日）
　前穂高―北尾根の最終絶壁に至る前に、短い鞍部の手前で東へ80ｍほど山狭を下りる。慎重さを要する斜登降で右（南）に向かい、草付きを越えてから、文字通り険しい壁に取り付く。岩棚まで壁を登ったら、平らなリンネを抜けて、斜め左上方にある大きなテラスまで進む。ここまでは中程度の難しさだが、大変砕けやすい。その後、壁はさらに険しくなり、岩石の色は明るさが増したように見える。テラスを右端まで進む（右手に小さな岩塔が見える）。そこから、斜め左にある短いチムニーまで岩壁を登る。チムニーを上方に抜けて、平易な場所まで登る。無事登頂。第2部は困難で砕けやすい。時間：壁の取り付きから3時間半

Ⅲ．屏風岩―北東ルート（第1リンネ・初直登。1934年8月17日）
　このルートでは、中央に高くそびえる巨大な岩柱の東側に

Bänder und Platten hinauf, bis ein Steilaufschwung zum weiteren Ausweichen nach links in einen überdachten Kamin zwingt. Dicht unterhalb des Daches führt ein Band aus ihm heraus; bald folgt ein zweiter, ähnlicher Kamin, den man durch ein Loch im Dach verläßt. Von seinem Ende nach rechts über dicht bewachsenes Gelände zurück zur Rinne, die hier in einem Felskessel endet (etwa halber Weg). Der Weiterweg führt leicht rechts aufwärts über eine lange Platteflucht bis zum höchste Punkt, von wo aus man einen kleinen Felskessel gelangt. In seinem Hintergrunde zieht ein überhängender Spalt empor. Wenige Meter rechts von ihm durch eine teilweise überhängende, brüchige Rinne zu einer Nische (Ring und Karabiner), dann Seiltraverse nach links zu dem erwähnten Spalt, der sich hier zum Kamin erweitert. In den empor zu einer Rinne (Ring), durch einen schrägen Spalt in der rechten Wand, zum Schluß nach rechts über die Wand erreicht man bewachsenes Gelände dicht unter dem Gipfelgrat.

★ Die Kletterei ist fast durchweg schwierig; im unteren Teil Reibungskletterei; der Aufstieg auf den kleinen Felskessel bis zum Gipfelgrat ist sehr schwer und brüchig. Zeiten: Einstieg bis Beginn der Plattenflucht 4 Std., bis zum kleinen Felskessel 1 Std, bis zum Gipfelgrat 2 Std (das letzte Stück nur etwa 40 m!) (Bei einer zweiten Begehung durch dieselben Teilnehmer im September desselben Jahres waren die Zeiten folgende: bis zum Beginn der Plattenflucht 2 1/2 Std., bis zum kleinen Felskessel 1 Std., bis zum Gipfelgrat 45 Minuten.) Der Abstieg erfolgt am besten, indem man durch Bergföhren und Rhododendrongestrüpp in etw. 1 Std. nach Süden zum höchsten Punkte des Grates steigt und dann in der nächsten Schlucht nach Westen zum Karasawa absteigt (eine Abseilstelle), wo man auf den Weg vom Yokoodani zur Hodakanokoya trifft.

<u>IV. Koyari, Südtraverse</u> (2.Begehung 22. VIII. 34)
Außer dem früher in diesem Buch beschriebenen Aufstiege über die Südostkante führt von der Schulter aus ein Quergang mit reizvollem Ausblick durch die ganze Südwand zur Westseite (auf die Schulter kann man auch

あるリンネを登る。横尾谷―岩小屋の辺りで渡渉するのが、壁に取り付く最善策だ。南岸を進み、ガレのリンネを通ると、1時間ほどで壁の取り付きに至る。最初の100mは、最も深いリンネの左側に沿って進み、滑りやすく険しい岩棚と扇岩テラスを越えて、垂直にそそり立つ絶壁の横まで登る。その先は、垂直の岩壁を左に迂回して、ひさしのようなチムニーの中を登らざるを得ない。その屋根状の岩の直下には岩棚が張り出している。同じようなチムニーが続くので、そのチムニーを伝いながら登る。チムニーを抜けると右に進み、草付きを通ってリンネに出る。リンネは岩のくぼみで終わる（ルートの約半分）。さらに少し右上方へ長い盤岩を越えて最高地点に至る。最高地点をさらに進むと小さな岩のくぼみに達する。その岩棚の背後にはオーバーハングの長い割れ目が上方へ延びている。そこから数メートル右へ進み、一部がオーバーハングになっている砕けやすい岩溝を通り、絶壁まで行く（リングとカラビナで）。そこからはザイルトラバースで、前述の長い割れ目まで左に進む。割れ目は幅が広がり、チムニーになる。そのチムニーを登り、リンネ（リングで）へ、右壁の斜めに走る長い割れ目を進み、最後に右側へ、壁を越えて草付きに達する。ここは頂上地点の直下に位置する。

★　登攀は一貫して困難である。下の方は摩擦を利用して登攀した。頂上までの小さな岩盤は非常に登りにくく砕けやすい。時間：取りつきは扇岩テラスの始まりまで4時間、小さな岩棚までは1時間、頂上の尾根までは2時間、（最後の登攀部分は約40mしかないが！）（2回目の登山は、同じ参加者で、同年の9月に行ったが、時間は次の通りである。扇岩テラスの始まりまで2時間半、小さな岩棚までは1時間、頂上尾根までは45分）。下山の最善ルートは以下の通り。ハイマツとツツジのやぶを通り、南へ約1時間で尾根の最高地点まで登り、それから次の峡谷を西に進む。沢へ下りると（懸垂下降部分）、横尾谷から穂高の小屋への道にぶつかる。

durch einen Riß links der südöstl. Kante gelangen): von der Schulter auf schmalem Bande nach links in die Südwand; schräg aufsteigend um eine Kante herum in eine Verschneidung. In ihr einige Meter absteigend zu einem Bande, das zunächst leicht abwärts, dann wieder ansteigend zu einer kleinen Scharte im Westgrat führt, von dort leicht zum Gipfel.

Teilnehmer an den Klettereien:
N.Wegelin S.F.A.C.
Chr. Hupfer D.Oe.A.V.

Kami Kochi Notes

There seem to be few remaining of those who climbed here 25 years and more ago. The motor buses and "electric factories" are certainly here, but they have not spoilt the mountains above.   There seem to be some early climbs & expeditions that have been omitted from this book!

In Aug 1913 Rev. W.H. & Mrs. Elwin, Miss Joynt & Rev. F. J. L. Macrae climbed Yakedake. This was before the eruption so the trees grew far up to the top and only a short way down from the lip of the crater was the grass killed by the fumes

★   In Aug. 1913 also, Miss Kathleen Hall, Alan R. Hall, Miss Hilda Buncombe

クライマーズ・ブック対訳

IV. 小槍、南壁トラバース（第2登攀②・1934年8月22日）

　前述の南東カンテ越えの登攀以外にも、山の肩からの斜登降では、魅力的な景観を楽しみながら、南壁全体を通って西側に抜けるルートがある。この山の肩では、南東カンテの左側にある裂け目を利用して登攀することも可能。山の肩から狭い岩棚の上を左側へ進み、南壁に至る。カンテを回り、切り立った岩壁を登る。コーナーを数メートルトラバースして岩棚に至る。岩棚をやや下方へ進み、再び西尾根の小さな短い鞍部を登る。そこからは楽に頂上へ。

難所を制覇した登攀者
ドイツ・オーストリア・アルペン連盟
N. ヴェーゲリン S.F.A.C
クリスティアン・フプファー

②87ページ②の経過もあり、「第2登攀」とは断じがたい。

1938.8

上高地メモ

　25年前にここから登った人は、今ではもうほとんど残っていないようだ。この地には現在バスが走り、「発電所」もあるが、だからといって高くそびえる山々の良さは失われてはいない。どうやら、この本には初期の登攀や遠征が一部抜けているようだ。①
　1913年8月には、W・H・エルウィン牧師夫妻、ジョイント女史、F・J・L・マクレー牧師が焼岳に登っている。噴火の前だったので、当時は山頂までずっと木が生い茂っており、火口の外輪付近の緑がガスでやられていただけだった。

①この指摘は鋭い。特に大きい脱落は1877年（78年説も）、お雇い外国人の英国人冶金技師W・ガウランドが、外国人として初めて槍を登頂し、「日本アルプス」と呼称したことだろう。

111

climbed Hodaka (presumably Mae Hodaka) leaving Kami Kochi in the morning, returned there, crossed the Tokugo Toge, walked to Shimazima thence to Matsumoto & reached Karuizawa at <u>midnight</u> the same day.

In July 1913 Immediately after climbing Ontake from Kiso Fukushima to summit in 1 day and returning to Agematsu the next day Miss Margaret Hall & Miss Hilda Buncombe walked from Akashina to Miyashiro at the foot of Ariakedake. Next day they climbed the then seldom used track up the front of Ariake and down to Nakabusa.

♥   They were the first women & first Europeans to climb this way. On the following day they climbed Tsubakuro by stream bed & monkey track & were possibly then the first European women to climb Tsubakuro. There was then no hut of any kind.

On Aug. 7th & 8th 1938 Rev. F. J. L. & Mrs. Macrae (nee Miss Margaret Hall) climbed Yari by the usual route and after a night at the Katano Hut climbed the Hodaka ridge to the Hodaka hut. The climb is done by so many that it was not remarkable except that an old man of 83 was met who had climbed to the Peak of Yari and a small boy of 3, wearing a tiny rucksack (!) was being carried up on a guide's back.

♠   An Austrian climber reported that white of egg rubbed into the eye will cure snow blindness in a day.

Returning after 25 years we again wish to acknowledge our indebtedness to those who blazed the trails and especially Mr. Weston, who lives now in loneliness in London since the death of Mrs. Weston in 1937

N. Margaret Macrae (nee Hall)
Fred John L Macrae

クライマーズ・ブック対訳

★ 同じ1913年8月にはキャサリン・ホール女史、アラン・R・ホール氏、ヒルダ・バンカム女史も朝のうちに上高地を出発し、穂高（おそらく前穂高）を登った。上高地に戻ると、徳本峠を越え、島々、松本まで歩き、その日の真夜中に軽井沢へ到着している。

1913年7月、マーガレット・ホール女史とヒルダ・バンカム女史が木曽福島から御嶽を登り、1日で登頂して、翌日上松に戻ると、その足で明科から有明岳麓の宮城まで歩いている。またその翌日、当時はめったに使う人がいない小道を通って有明まで登り、中房へと下った。

♥ 2人はこのルートで登山した最初の女性であり、最初の欧州人だ。翌日、沢沿いと獣道を伝い、燕に登っている。おそらく、燕を登った欧州人女性としても初だろう。当時、その辺りに小屋の類いは一切なかった。

1938年8月7日と8日の両日、F・J・L・マクレー牧師がマーガレット夫人（旧姓ホール）を伴い、通常のルートで槍に登る。肩の小屋で1泊して、穂高小屋を目指し穂高の尾根を伝った。今では非常に多くの人が登攀するルートなので、特筆すべきことといえば、途中で槍の登攀を終えた83歳の男性に会ったこと、小さなリュックサックを背負った3歳の男の子（！）が山案内人におぶわれていたのを見たことくらいだろう。

♠ オーストリア人登山者の話によれば、卵の白身を目にこすりつけると、1日で雪目が治るらしい。

25年ぶりに戻り、先鞭をつけてくださった皆さんにもう一度お礼を伝えたい。特に、1937年、夫人に先立たれ、ロンドンで寂しく暮らしておられるウェストン氏には心から感謝申し上げる。

N・マーガレット・マクレー（旧姓ホール）
フレッド・ジョン・L・マクレー

②有明とは、神話や安曇節で知られる有明山（2,269m）のこと。この女性パーティーは1913年に黒川沢経由で登頂し、翌日は中房温泉から小屋ができる以前の燕岳にも登っている。快挙である（案内人の有無は不明）。

On Aug. , 1940 the following party arrived here on the way home to Karuizawa from a week-end at Lake Nojiri.

Alberta Tann — Hiroshima
Thelma Fish —   "
Mildred Hudgins — Kobe
Mary Mac Millan — Hiroshima
Patricia Mc Hugh — Tetsugen, Chosen
Fusa Nagai — Hiroshima
Elda Daniels — Kainei, Chosen

One day was spent in a climb to Tokomoto Toge and although we were not professional climbers equipped with ropes and picks there was the same anticipation of the goal. Not only the hectic ride on an ever-crowded bus the previous day but also the steep upgrade resulted in weary limbs and aching backs and moanful sighs. But all this was compensated for the numerous woodsy scents, the shy charm of the alpine flowers (by actual count 28 varieties found) and distant bird-calls that elated us.

A particular pleasure of the trip was reading the account of the Volcanic Eruption of 1915 as recorded in this book by J. Merle Davis, after which a visit to the lake mentioned took on added interest.

クライマーズ・ブック対訳

1940.8

　1940年8月　日※、週末を野尻湖で過ごした後、軽井沢に戻る途中で上高地に立ち寄りました。パーティーは次のメンバーです。

※原文でも日は空欄になっている。

　　アルバータ・タン　―　広島
　　テルマ・フィッシュ　―　広島
　　ミルドレッド・ハッジンズ　―　神戸
　　メアリー・マク・ミラン　―　広島
　　パトリシア・マク・フュー　―　朝鮮・テツゲン
　　フサ・ナガイ　―　広島
　　エルダ・ダニエルズ　―　朝鮮・カイネイ

　1日がかりで徳本峠（トクモト）まで登りました。私たちはロープやピッケルを装備した登山のプロではありませんが、目的地にたどり着きたいという思いは同じです。前日のバスが大混雑で大変だったうえに登りも険しく、身体がクタクタになりました。腰が痛み、思わずうめき声が出てしまうほどです。とはいえ、芳しい森の香り、かれんに咲く高山の花々の美しさ（実際に数えたところ、28種見つかりました）、遠くに聞こえる鳥のさえずりから元気をもらえたので、苦労が報われました。
　今回の旅で特に良かったのは、J・メルル・デイヴィスがこの本に残した1915年の噴火の記述を読めたことです。おかげで、件（くだん）の池を訪れたときもがぜん興味が湧きました。

On Aug. 30th 1940
Yesterday I walked to the
Yake-Dake (very interesting!). Tomorrow
I intend to climb the Oku-Hodaka

Karol Staniszewski
Secretary of the Polish Embassy
in Tokio
member of the POLISH MOUNTAINEER club

7 septembre 1946

    En reprenant ce livre après 6 années d'interruption ,
ces quelques lignes sont non pas pour décrire une première
intéressante ni pour ajouter quelque détail sur une ascension,
mais simplement pour affirmer l'intérêt des Alpes japonaises
pour l'alpiniste , pour le rochassier même exigeant

R Establie C a 7

1940.8

1940年8月30日

昨日、焼岳まで歩いた(とてもおもしろかった!)。明日は奥穂高(ホダカ)に登るつもりだ。

在京駐日ポーランド大使館書記官
ポーランド山岳会会員
キャロル・スタニスツースキー

1946.9(仏)

1946年9月7日

　6年後に、このブックに書き加えたいものがあります。単なる登山についての新しい発見、あるいは山に関しての詳しい情報ではありません。ここで、あらためて強調したいのは、経験豊な登山者でさえ、日本アルプスはすばらしいということです。

R Establie C a 7

Covering 28 June - 5 July 1947
5 July 1947

Trail notes (going back to Mr. Weston's 2nd paragraph suggestion):
1. Shimizuya to Tokusawa — reasonably good except for some marshy sections — practically a boulevard most of the way. Very pleasant easy going, with good views of Myojin, Mae- and Oku-Hodaka, and Nishi-Hodaka.
2. Tokusawa to Yokoo — Some slides, with detours up and around them. Many bridges of rotten logs — best to detour if not apparently safe.
3. Yokoo-dani to Ichinomata — same as (2).
4. Bridge on Yari trail 200 meters beyond Ichinomata is out.
    "   " Jonen-Dake trail abt. 1 Km reported out or impossible.
    " s " from Yokoo to start of Karasawa trail all out.
5. Trail up Nishi Hodaka from Shimizuya poorly marked, but from snow patches on, follow new small blazes. Nishi-Hodaka hut (just above forest and below scrub pine) in very good shape.
6. Otaki-dake trail — goes up right bank of river from Tokusawa instead of left as shown on 1931 survey maps 1:50,000. Single log bridges over stream.
7. Yake-dake trail — in very good shape — easily in 3 hours — hut at saddle.
8. Cessation of rain for several days (it has been raining almost constantly) will reduce or eliminate many of the obstacles above.

   — Have enjoyed my visit immensely, altho turned back from several climbs by flood waters & lack of bridges.
   Hitori desu. Chuck Bowden チャルス ボーデン

クライマーズ・ブック対訳

1947.7

1947年7月5日
6月28日から7月5日まで

登山の記録（ウェストン氏の2段落目の提案に対して）：
1. 清水屋から徳沢：沼のような場所が一部あったが、それ以外は良好。道はほとんどが大通りのように広い。とても快適で歩きやすく、明神、前・奥穂高（ホダカ）、西穂高の絶景が望める。
2. 徳沢から横尾：数ヵ所崩落、迂回路あり。多くの橋で丸太が朽ちていた。安全が確認できない限り、迂回すべき。
3. 横尾谷から一ノ俣：(2) に同じ。
4. 槍の登山道で、一ノ俣から200 mのところにある橋が外れている。
   常念岳の登山道①で、1kmのところにある橋が外れている、もしくは、通過不可との情報あり。
   横尾から涸沢の登山道の始点まで、すべての橋が外れている。
5. 西穂高の山道は清水屋から目印がほとんどないが、雪の残る辺りから真新しい小さな目印が続く。西穂高小屋（森のちょうど上、ハイマツの下）は状態が非常に良い。
6. 大滝岳の登山道：徳沢から、1931年調査の5万分の1地形図に記されている川の左岸ではなく、右岸を登る。渓流に丸太を1本渡しただけの橋が複数見られる。
7. 焼岳の登山道：非常に良好（3時間あれば十分）鞍部に小屋あり。
8. 数日間雨がやめば（これまでのところ、ほとんど雨が続いている）、上記の問題の多くは解消、もしくは軽減されるだろう。

①一ノ俣から常念岳への登山路は、特に下部が難路。一時期、岩壁に針金を張り巡らせていた。現在は廃道。

5 July 1947

  Chuichi Hasegawa-san, Chief of the Forestry Office, Matsumoto, with 2 of his colleagues, Ōkubo-san & Moteu-san, and my friend Masato (Mike) Okuhara-san were kind enough to visit me here for an informal discussion with a view to improving the safety of the trails, making trail signs and markers, and making available up-to-date maps and information for climbers in the Hida region. New maps (1:25,000) (in Kanji only) are being prepared and will soon be available, presumably at Matsumoto and Shimizuya. I suggested he write the Col. Mtn. Club, D.O.C., A.M.C., G.M.C., who would probably be glad to send detailed information supplementing my few suggestions. Zoe Beraud & I were forced to descend a water course last night due to insufficient markings on the Nishi-Hodaka-Shimizuya trail.

C.B. Bowden　チャルス・ボーデン

――川の水があふれていたり、橋がなくなっていたりで、引き返さなければならないことが度々あったものの、非常に楽しい滞在だった。

ヒトリデス。

チャック・ボーデン　チャルス・ボーデン※　　　　　　　　　　　※日本語署名

1947年7月5日

　松本の営林局長ハセガワ・チュウイチさんと同僚のオオクボさん、モテウさんの両名、それに私の友人オクハラ・マサト（マイク）さんがわざわざ会いに足を運んでくれた。登山道の安全向上、目印や道しるべの設置、飛騨地域の登山者が利用できる最新版の地図や情報の準備などについてざっくばらんに意見を交わす。新しい地図（2万5,000分の1）（漢字のみ）は現在作成中で、近いうちにおそらく松本と清水屋で入手できるようになるだろう。ハセガワさんには、コロラド・マウンテン・クラブ、D・O・C、A・M・C、G・M・Cに一筆書くよう提案した。私のアドバイスを補完する細かなことを喜んで教えてくれるはずだ。西穂高と清水屋を結ぶ登山道には目印が少なく、ゾーイ・ベロー②と私は昨晩、川を伝って下山せざるを得なかった。

②進駐軍で富士山に登頂した最初の女性。

C・B・ボーデン　チャルス・ボーデン※　　　　　　　　　　　※日本語署名

5 - 9 Sept. 1947

Spent three days on Nishi-Dake, investigating the alpine fauna. Hut comfortable, trails excellent, but all wildlife lamentably scarce.

Oliver L. Austin, Jr.
Head, Wildlife Branch
NRS, GHQ, SCAP

16 August 1948

With many thanks to Mr. Iijima for having afforded me this rare opportunity to visit this, one of the most scenic spots in Japan. I am by no means a mountain-climber, having lived most of my life in a big city. The exotic beauty of the Japanese Alps, however, has inspired me to the point that, had I more time to spend in this area, I would have joined some group of climbers in order to appreciate the real wonders and beautiful sights of this unique mountain range.

In these days of continued diplomatic bickering throughout the world, one can't help but stop to think and appreciate the serenity, wholesomeness, hospitable atmosphere of Kamikochi.

Crescenzo F. Guida
Capt. Inf., Govt. Sec., GHQ

クライマーズ・ブック対訳

1947.9

1947年9月5日〜9日

　西岳で3日間過ごし、高山植物の調査を行った。小屋は快適で、登山道もすばらしいが、野生生物は嘆かわしいほど少なかった。

連合国最高司令官総司令部天然資源局
野生生物課　課長
オリバー・L・オースチン・ジュニア

1948.8

1948年8月16日

　貴重な機会をくださったイイジマ氏に深く感謝したい。日本でも特にすばらしい景観を持つこの土地を訪れることができたのは、イイジマ氏のおかげだ。人生の大半を都会で過ごしてきた私は、いわゆる登山家では決してないが、日本アルプスはあまりに美しく、ここで過ごせる時間がもっとあったのなら、この山々が持つ真の驚異と美を見んがために、きっとどこかのパーティーに加わっていただろうと思う。
　世界中で国同士のいざこざが絶えない今日、上高地の静けさや健やかさ、温かさには自然と足が止まり、そのありがたさが心にしみるものだ。

GHQ民政局、歩兵連隊大尉
クレシェンゾ・F・グイーダ

To Mr. Kato, 30 July 1949

To the very lucky ones who have visited this very beautiful spot and to the many very lucky ones who will follow me may I say that of all the beautiful places in the world "God" blessed this wonder land long before the other spots throughout the world. I wish Mr. Kato, may, with good health, remain here for many long years.

Robert Hall
Great Neck, L.I.
New York

30 July 1949

"Lift up thine eyes unto the hills whence thy strength cometh." Mountains have been always a source of inspiration for me since my boyhood. I am certainly grateful to be here among the famous peaks of so-called "the ceiling of Japan."

David Y. Takahara
Lake Nojiri

クライマーズ・ブック対訳

1949.7

1949年7月30日　加藤さま

　この大変美しい場所を訪れたことのあるとても幸運な皆さん、そして、これから訪れる、とても幸運な大勢の皆さんにお伝えしたいのは、「神」は世界にあまたある美しい場所にも先んじて、このすばらしい土地に、恵みを与えたのだということです。加藤さんが今後も健康に留意され、当地で末永くご活躍されることをお祈りいたします。

ニューヨーク州
ロングアイランド、グレートネック
ロバート・ホール

1949.7

1949年7月30日

「目を上げて、山々を仰ぎみよ。汝(なんじ)の力が生まれしところを」。山は、幼い頃から私のインスピレーションの源だ。「日本の天井」と呼ばれるこの有名な峰群の中でも、特にここに来られたことは非常にありがたい。

野尻湖
デイビッド・Y・タカハラ

To Mr. Kato: Kamikochi is one of the beauty spots of the world. The rugged beauty of the peaks will always remain in my memory.

Mountain climbing is not my forte, but photographically these mountains will be surpassed by few senic spots.

The trip to Kami Kochi was thoroughly enjoyed with only one regret the stay was not of sufficient duration to enjoy the mountain splendor to the fullest extent. Mr. Kato was an excellent host. May he have many more years in which to build this beauty spot into a place for many to enjoy.

Ellis J. Kohler
Lincoln Nebr.
30 July 1949

September 6th - 11th
1953

There have been no accounts written during the last few years. So it would appear that I am the first member of the British Commonwealth Forces, which are based for the most part at Kure in support of the Division fighting (until one month ago) in Korea, to visit this lovely distinct. This I can scarcely believe, but I am pleased, although I have made no historic ascents or routes, to be the first of these forces to make a record in this book of a visit, which,

クライマーズ・ブック対訳

1949.7

加藤さま

　上高地はまさに世界有数の景勝地です。鋭い峰々の美しさは、いつまでも私の記憶に残ることでしょう。
　登山は得意ではありませんが、これほど絵になる山々はそうないでしょう。
　今回の上高地への旅は大いに楽しめました。唯一心残りなのは、滞在期間が十分ではなく、山のすばらしさを思う存分楽しめなかったことです。加藤さんのもてなしは最高でした。加藤さんが今後もますますご健勝で、この景勝地を多くの人々が楽しめる場所にされることをお祈りいたします。

1949年7月30日
ネブラスカ州リンカーン
エリス・J・コーラー

1953.9

1953年
9月6日〜11日

　この数年間、何も書き込まれていない。どうやらイギリス連邦占領軍（1ヵ月前まで韓国で交戦中だった師団の支援で、大半は呉に駐屯している）で、このすてきな地方を訪れたのは私が初めてのようだ。にわかに信じられないが、歴史的な登攀をしたわけでも、新しいルートを登ったわけでもないのに、占領軍初の人物として、たとえ短いものであれ、日韓滞

although too short, has been a highlight of my tour in Japan and Korea.

My first day here was cloudy with scattered showers and I climbed Yakedake to admire the multicoloured rocks and stones with the issuing vapours. On the summit I was surprised to meet Proff. and Dr. Weber from Mount Vernon, New York, a meeting which shows that Kamikochi, thanks to the sterling work of earlier pioneers, is becoming comparatively well known.

My ambition was fired by the sight of the cloud capped peaks of Yarikatake and Hodaka to the north and the next day, with Mr. Ushimaru Fukumi as guide, I set out, on a hot, cloudless morning, for the main range.

★ By the banks of the Asakusa we fell in with Sgt. Rodney Lingard, of the Australian Army, and Mr. Tanigawa Katsumi, with whom we were to journey companionably for the next few days.

The ascent of Yari was arduous and uneventful but we were rewarded by a magnificent sunset from the top of the peak and a spectacular 'Spectre of the Brocken.' Yari threw a perfectly symmetrical, narrow, conical shadow, sharply delineated and etched with a golden luminosity, from the base to the top of the clouds piled up in the Kamikochi valley and on the summit of this cone, an almost completely circular halo vividly surrounded the well defined, enormous figures of each one of us.

♥ Sunrise, as seen from the summit was equally splendid. From a level sea of clouds, stained red and gold towards the East, rose Asama, Yatsugatake, Fujiyama, Kai-komagateke, Shirane, Kiso-Komagatake, Ontake, Norikura, Hakusan and nearer the jagged crests and cliffs of Hodaka. All the peaks of Central Japan were visible in this magnificent panorama.

We traversed that day along the ridge from Yari to Hodaka-goya. This is an interesting route, especially between Minami-dake and Kitahotadake where there are several moderately difficult rock pitches and exposed aretes; all the time, in good weather such as we had, there are wonderful views, both to the East and West. We took, travelling at a leisurely pace, about nine hours.

♠ The route we followed the next day up Oku-Hodaka, across to Mae

在中の格別な思い出となった今回の上高地訪問について、この本に記録を残せることをうれしく思う。

　ここに来た初日は曇り模様で、雨が降ったりやんだりしていた。焼岳に登り、さまざまな色の岩石と、その隙間から噴き出す蒸気に目を奪われた。山頂で、ニューヨーク州マウントバーノン出身の教授、ドクター・ウェバーにばったり出会ったのには驚いた。こうした出会いは、これまでの先達のすばらしい取り組みの結果、多少なりとも上高地の名が知られてきた証拠に他ならない。

　私の熱い思いに火がついたのは、雲をかぶった槍ヶ岳(ヤリガタケ)と穂高(ホダカ)の頂を北の方角に見つけたときだった。翌日、雲一つない暑い朝、山の案内人牛丸福美(うしまるふくみ)氏とともに連峰を目指して出発した。

★　アサクサ川①の岸近くで、オーストラリア軍のロドニー・リンガード軍曹とタニガワ・カツミ氏に偶然出会った。この２人とは、それからの数日間、ともに旅を楽しむことになる。

　槍の登攀はただひたすらつらいだけだったが、その苦労は報われた。山頂から雄大な夕焼けを望めただけでなく、息を飲むような「ブロッケン現象」も見られたのだ。上高地の谷に幾重にも重なった雲の上に、完全に左右対称な細い円すい形をした槍の影が落ち、輪郭は金色に輝く光でくっきりと浮かび上がる。その円すいの頂点では、ほとんど真円といえる光輪が、私たち１人ひとりの巨大な黒々とした影を包み込んでいた。

♥　山頂から見る日の出も負けず劣らずすばらしい。水平に広がる雲海の東側が赤と金に染まり、浅間や八ヶ岳、富士山(フジヤマ)、甲斐駒ヶ岳、白根、木曽駒ヶ岳、御嶽、乗鞍、白山、手前には穂高の切り立った峰や岩壁が姿を現す。実にすばらしい眺めで、中部日本の峰々を一望できた。

　その日は槍から穂高小屋に向けて尾根沿いにトラバースした。これはおもしろいルートで、南岳と北穂高岳(キタホタダケ)の間は適度

①次ページにも出てくるが、「アサクサ川」は「梓川」の間違い。

Hodaka and down the steep slopes to Kamikochi is not as interesting, although the views of the Kamikochi valley and the long trail through the woods are very lovely.

I should have liked to do some rock climbing — especially on that remarkable gendarme at the base of the peak of Yari, but, to my disappointment, no ropes, or eager companions, were available.

At the risk of being repetitions, I should remind readers that, except at the huts, there is no water on the ridge. The trail is well marked, and with moderate experience, a map and good weather, a guide is not essential - although I found Mr. Ushimaru Fukumi at all times a pleasant and reliable companion. The huts are comfortable but I found that my appetite becomes fickle in the mountains and I was unable to face, never mind eat, the rice, which I enjoy in the plains, that is available. For those that might feel the same, I advise carrying some European-type food.

◆ After the strenuous efforts in the mountains, the joys of relaxing in the hot springs, of listening and seeing the Asakusa rushing through the birch forest, and of the hospitality and comforts of the Shimazuya, are great rewards for any visitor to Kamikochi.

Michael Ashcroft
Capt. R.A.M.C.
10.9.53

に難しい岩場やむき出しのやせ尾根が続き、特に楽しめた。私たちのように天候に恵まれれば、東にも西にも常に見事な景観が望める。のんびりとしたペースで進んだので、9時間ほどかかった。

♠　翌日は奥穂高に登り、前穂高まで縦走して上高地への急斜面を下ったのだが、前日ほどはおもしろくなかった。ただ、上高地の渓谷の景色と、樹林帯の登山道はとてもすてきだった。

　自分としては岩登りを体験したかった。特に、槍の穂先の基部にある、あのすばらしい岩峰にチャレンジしたかったのだが、残念なことに、ロープもなければ、熱心に誘ってくれる仲間もいなかった。

　繰り返しになるのは承知で皆さんに注意喚起したいのが、小屋以外に、尾根には水場がないということだ。トレイルには目印がしっかりある。それなりの経験と地図があり、好天に恵まれていれば、案内人は必要とは限らない。とはいえ、今回案内をしてくれた牛丸福美氏は感じがよく、信頼できると思う。小屋は快適だが、山に登ると食欲にムラが出ることが分かった。小屋にある米も、平地ではおいしく食べられるのだが、山では食べるどころか見ることさえできなかった。不安に思う人は、欧州で食べているようなものを持参することをお勧めする。

♦　山での奮闘後に温泉につかってリラックスしたり、カバの森林でアサクサ川①のせせらぎを楽しんだり、清水屋(シマズヤ)の温かいもてなしと居心地の良さを味わったりする楽しみは、上高地を訪れる人にとってこの上ない褒美である。

①前ページ参照。

1953年9月10日
英国陸軍医療部隊大尉
マイケル・アッシュクロフト

30 July 1954

As the first American here in quite some time, I'd like to add my quick comments about a very fine one weeks trip in the Japan Alps with a wonderful Japanese friend. We started one week ago by climbing up Shirouma and then over Shirouma, Yari and down to the bus stop. The climb was wonderful — beautiful snow fields, gorgeous Alpine flowers, and magnificent Alpine sunshine. The hut near the summit of Shirouma was very good and everyone very kind.

After Shirouma, we headed for Ariake on the train, then up to Enzan-so and another fine night in the high country of Japan. The weather, however, was not in as good a humor as our spirits, as it began to rain and it has been doing just that for the past three days. After Enzan-so we headed over to Yari, up Yari yesterday in a heavy downpour of rain, then down here to Kamikochi and soon back to Tokyo.

★   To me the Japan Alps are mountains of rare beauty and have a special place in the mountains of the world. In comparison with the U.S., the Japan Alps have a certain extra-rugged beauty, and of course the popularity of climbing over here helps a lot to bring this beauty closer to the people. I hope soon to return and tramp again through the high country of Japan

William W. Biddle   U.S. Army
D.O.C., Appalachian Trail Conference
Radnor, Pennsylvania

クライマーズ・ブック対訳

1954.7

1954年7月30日

　この地に米国人が立ち寄ったのは随分と久しぶりなので、すばらしい日本人の友と過ごした1週間の極上の旅について、少し書き残したい。私たち2人の旅は1週間前、白馬(シロウマ)の登山から始まった。白馬岳と白馬鑓ヶ岳(やりがたけ)を越えて、バス停まで下りた。今回の登山はすばらしかった。美しい雪原、色あでやかに咲き誇る高山の花々、見事な輝きを放つ高山の日の光。白馬の頂上近くにある小屋はとても快適で、皆とても親切だった。

　白馬のあとは電車で有明に向かって燕山荘まで登り、日本の山でまたすてきな一晩を過ごした。しかしながら、空は私たちほどご機嫌ではなかったようで、いったん降り出した雨は、それから3日間やむ気配を見せなかった。燕山荘を後にして槍に向かい、昨日、大雨の中を槍に登頂、それからここ上高地まで下りてきた。間もなく東京に戻る。

★　私に言わせれば、日本アルプスは類まれなる美しい山々であり、世界の山の中でも特別な存在だ。米国の山と比べると、日本アルプスには極めて険しい尖峰が持つ独特の美しさがある。もちろん、日本の登山人気のおかげで、この美しさがより身近なものになっているのは言うまでもない。またすぐにこの地に戻り、日本の高地を歩き回りたいと思う。

ペンシルベニア州ラドナー
D・O・C、アパランチアン・トレイル・カンファレンス
米国陸軍
ウィリアム・W・ビドル

27 June 1955

Apparently we are the first Americans here in the 1955 season. A party consisting of Colonels Peter Allen and Samuel Hall of the U.S. Army and Mr. Max Schmutter of the American Consulate began to climb Mt. Mishiyokada at 0845 hours today. This slope is certainly a beautiful work of nature, at least for the first half of the climb. At this point I returned to the hotel, leaving the other to continue. Perhaps I shall climb the top half this afternoon, but I rather doubt it.

George I. Mulhern, Jr.
Boston, Mass.

16th September 1957

Four people have reached the Shimizuya Inn after spending 3 days in the high peaks. We started from Yokohama & travelled by train via Shinjuku, to Matsumoto, Ariake. From there by taxi to Nakabusa Onsen. There we stayed the first night. Next morning we left the Inn at 6.20 & walked up & up through the woods to Hutte Enzaso which we reached at 10.25. After a cup of Jap. tea & rest we went on to Akaywadake (1 pm) & on to Hut Otenjo (1.30) where we rested for 1 hour. Reached hutte Nishitake at 4.30, where

クライマーズ・ブック対訳

1955.6

1955年6月27日

　どうやら私たちは、1955年登山シーズンで一番乗りした米国人のようだ。パーティーのメンバーは米国陸軍のピーター・アレン大佐、サミュエル・ホール大佐、米国領事館のマックス・シュマッター氏で、今朝8時45分、ミシヨカダ山①の登山を開始した。この山の斜面はまさに自然の造形美だ。少なくとも登攀の半分までは。というのも、私は登攀を続行するメンバーを後にして、1人で宿に戻ってきたからだ。午後にはあらためて頂上までの残り半分を登ろうかとも思うが、どうなることやら。

①西穂高のことだと思われる。

マサチューセッツ州ボストン
ジョージ・I・マルハーン・ジュニア

1957.9

1957年9月16日

　連峰で3日間過ごしたあと、清水屋に到着。私たち4人は横浜から新宿を経由して松本、有明まで列車で来た。有明から中房温泉までタクシーで移動。最初の晩は中房で宿泊した。翌朝、宿を6時20分に出て、樹林帯を抜けて上へ上へと燕山荘（エンザソウ）まで登山を続ける。小屋に着いたのは10時25分。日本茶で一息ついてから赤岩岳に向けて出発する（午後1時）。大天井小屋に立ち寄り（1時30分）、1時間休憩した。

135

we stayed. All day we had sunshine & clear-cut views of all the mountains, including Fuji-san. Second day we left hut at 6.20 & took 3 hours to reach Katadake Hutte. There we left our rucsacs & climbed to the very top of the Spear of Yari. This was an interesting scramble & rock-climb of 30 minutes. Returned to hut &, after having some food, collected our rucsacs & set off for the Hodaka range. We reached Kita-Hodaka-Hutte at 5.15, all very tired. (It should be noted that we took a very long time over this 2nd section, due to two aged members of the party feeling very weary. It should also be noted that the other two members were very patient & encouraging!)

★ Next day we proceeded in leisurely fashion & brilliant sunshine to Karasawa & Takasawa, & on the following day gently walked to Kami-Kochi. As we reached this Inn the rain began & it looks as if it will never cease. But we were welcomed in by the owner & made so comfortable that the weather doesn't matter at the moment. Tomorrow? Yes; but now all we wish to enjoy are the hot baths.

During the whole route the paths were well-marked & the weather perfect. No one could have seen the Japanese Alps so clearly & under such ideal conditions as we did. Travelling "out of season" is well worth while. Check up beforehand as to whether or not a Hutte is open. Carry some European food, such as bread. Carry some water or fruit juice. Then the rest lies in your own powers.

♥ Our Japanese guide, interpreter & mountain climber of some note planned our route & we had no difficulties. He smoothed the way in the huts in explaining our wants. He was always helpful & kind.

If we may make a suggestion for future use, we think that if the signposts would be given in English as well as in Japanese, it would be extremely helpful to the foreigner travelling without a guide.

A.H. Goodliffe (British)
Kathleen Goodliffe (")
Peter Goodliffe (15 years   ")

クライマーズ・ブック対訳

　4時30分、ヒュッテ西岳に到着、そこで宿を取る。終日、太陽に恵まれ、富士山も含めすべての山々がはっきりと見えた。2日目、小屋を6時20分に出発、3時間かけてカタダケ小屋①に到着する。そこにリュックサックを置いて、槍の穂先に登った。岩を相手に格闘した30分の登攀はおもしろかった。小屋に戻り、軽く食べ物を取り、リュックサックを持って穂高(ホダカ)連峰へと出発した。北穂高小屋に着いたのは5時15分。皆くたびれ果てていた。（特筆すべきは、この2日目の行程が長時間にわたったことだ。年長の2人が疲労困憊(こんぱい)に陥ったせいである。残る2人がとても辛抱強くつきあい、一生懸命元気づけてくれたことも記しておこう）

①槍の「肩ノ小屋」、現在の槍ヶ岳山荘のこと。

★　翌日、すばらしい日差しを受けながら、のんびりと涸沢、タカサワ②まで進み、その翌日にはゆっくり歩いて上高地に到着した。この宿に着いた頃に雨が降り始め、今もまるでやみそうにない。しかし、宿の主に温かく迎えられ、とても居心地がよかったので、天気のことなど気にならなくなった。明日は？　もちろん気になる。でも、今何よりも4人が望んでいるのは、熱い湯船につかることだ。

②北穂高小屋から涸沢を経て徳沢で泊まったとみられる。

　ルートはどの道にも分かりやすい目印があり、天候も非の打ちどころがなかった。これだけ理想的な条件で、これほどはっきりと日本アルプスを眺めることができた人は今までにきっといないだろう。「季節外れ」に旅するだけの価値は十分にある。山小屋が開いているかどうかは、前もって調べておくこと。パンなどヨーロッパの食べ物をいくらか持っていくとよい。水やフルーツジュースを携帯しよう。あとはあなたの実力次第だ。

♥　私たちの案内をしてくれた日本人は通訳者、登山家として多少知られる人物だ。彼がルートを計画してくれたおかげで、一切問題なく過ごすことができた。小屋でも不便なく過ごせたのは、彼が私たちの希望を説明してくれたからだ。いつも親切で、たくさん助けてもらった。

Jun Yamakawa (Japanese)

Sound of flute
has returned
to bamboo
forest

These mountains offer us pure air, clear water, green verdure.
They help us uncrowd and un-don't and quiet our mind in the Mind of Great Nature.
So we are purified and healed just by being here —-

Paul Reps
September 20, 1959

クライマーズ・ブック対訳

　今後のために一つ提案させてもらうなら、道しるべに日本語だけでなく英語も表記されていれば、案内人を伴わずに登山する外国人がとても助かるのではないかと思う。

A・H・グッドリフ（英国人）
キャサリーン・グッドリフ（〃）
ピーター・グッドリフ（15歳　〃）
ジュン・ヤマカワ（日本人）

③記録に地名の誤記が目立つのも、英語での標識がなかったせいか。最近は英語、韓国語、中国語の標識、地図も広まった。

1959.9

笛の音が竹の林に戻ってきた

　この山々は、澄みわたる風と清らかな水、緑豊かな草木を与えてくれる。
　大いなる自然の御心(みこころ)にあって、何ものにも惑わされず、負の考えを拭い去り、心を静める助けとなる。
　それゆえ、ただここにいるだけでわれわれの心は洗われ、癒やされるのだ

1959年9月20日
ポール・レプス

24th October 1960

Fred Lakin   Hobart, Tasmania, Aust
Shigeo Nakagawa   Hitotubashi University Alpine Club
Shinji Kobayasi

We have visited the Shimizu-ya after climbing Mt Yake under the most perfect conditions. Tomorrow we leave Kamikochi to climb for 4 days in the Hotaki Range & Yari, returning to Kamikochi. This must be the most beautiful time of the year at Kamikochi & I think the Japan Alps should receive much more attention by Foreign visitors, as they compare most favorably with the Austria Alps or the Canadian Rockies.

F.N. Lakin

Hotel Shimizuya
May 24-25-26, 1962

It is with pleasure that we have read the notable and historic accounts of climbing in the Japan Alps as contained in this record book. In Japan, as in America, the ramparts of wilderness beauty, are becoming diminished by the encroachment of "civilization." May the Japanese people have the foresight to preserve these beautiful mountain areas, unchanged, for the enjoyment of

クライマーズ・ブック対訳

```
1960.10
```

1960年10月24日
オーストラリア　タスマニア州ホバート
フレッド・レイキン
一橋大学山岳会　シゲオ・ナカガワ
　　　　　　　　シンジ・コバヤシ

　最高のコンディションで焼岳に登頂した後、清水屋を訪れる。明日には上高地を出て、4日かけて穂高連峰(ホタキ)と槍を登攀し、また上高地に戻ってくる予定だ。上高地はきっと今が1年で最も美しい時期にちがいない。日本アルプスはオーストリアのアルプスやカナディアン・ロッキーと比べても全く遜色ないのだから、もっと外国人から注目されてしかるべきだ。

F・N・レイキン

```
1962.5
```

清水屋旅館にて
1962年5月24日、25日、26日

　この宿帳にあるような日本アルプス登攀の注目すべき歴史的記録を読むことができて喜ばしく思う。現在日本でも米国同様、大自然の美しい城壁である峡谷が「文明」の侵略によって失われつつある。日本の人々に先見の明(めい)があり、この美しい山岳地帯をこれまでと変わらない姿で、未来の世代が享

future generations.

A walk to Tokugo Toge afforded a magnificent view of the spires of Hodakayama opposite. It is our impression that the snow pack is relatively light for this time of year.

James and Sue Higman
Santa Barbara, California
Life member,
Sierra Club

19 to 26 Sept 1962
Thomas L. Johnston and wife, Helene
Alpine Club of Canada and Sierra Club of Calif.

Following notes on climbing in this area based on experience of writer, present trails, Koyas etc may be of interest to other climbers in this area. Note that gradation of climbs is based on following scale of severity. Classes 1 and 2: rock scrambling; Class 3: ropes advisable if members of party are relatively inexperienced, climbing is continuous (without belay); Class 4: severe climbing ropes required, belays required; Class 5: Extension of 4th class piton technique necessary; Class 6 vertical climbing (rock engineering)

1. <u>Nishi Hodaka</u>, class 2, on pinnacles, 4 1/2 hrs ascent 3 hrs descent. clear and cold
2. <u>Oku Hodaka</u>, Class 2 (above koya), 4 1/2 hrs Kamikochi to Karisawa koya; thence 2 1/2 hrs summit. (20 min Hodaka Koya to summit). Descent 3 hrs to Yakoo Sanso Koya, thence 2 hrs to Kamikochi, cloudy and cold

受できるように保存してくれることを願うばかりだ。
　徳本峠まで歩くと、穂高山(ホダカヤマ)の峰々の雄大な姿を向かい側に拝むことができた。この時期にしては積雪が比較的少ないというのが私たちの印象だ。

カリフォルニア州サンタバーバラ
ジェームズ＆スー・ヒグマン夫妻
シエラクラブ
終身会員

```
                                                            1962.9
```

1962年9月19日～26日
カナダ山岳会、シエラクラブ・カリフォルニア州支部
トーマス・L・ジョンストン、妻ヘレン①

①L・ジョンストン、妻ヘレン（夫妻）は、高いレベルの登山家と思われる。以下のルートの格付け、夫妻の登破時間は欧米人ならではのタイム。

　この一帯の登山に関して、筆者の経験や現在のトレイル、小屋など、ここの山を登る他の人たちの参考になりそうな事柄を記録に残していく。なお、登山の格付けは以下の難易度を基準とする。
クラス1＆2：岩登り。／クラス3：パーティーのメンバーが比較的経験の浅い場合、ロープがあった方がよい。登りが続く（ビレー不要）。／クラス4：ロープ必須、ビレー必須となる難しい登攀。／クラス5：クラス4の上。ピトンを打てるテクニックが必要。／クラス6：垂直登攀（岩を制する技術）
1. 西穂高(ホダカ)：山頂までクラス2。登り4時間半、下り3時間。快晴、寒い。

3. <u>Oku Hodaka</u> — <u>Nishi Hodaka</u> Traverse. 3rd class — 5 hours. Loose rock.
4. <u>Yari</u>; class 2 on main pinnacle above Koya. (class 3 & 4 routes possible) 6 1/2 hours from Kamikochi to Yari Koya thence 20 minutes to summit. Descent 6 hours. Clear & cold.
5. <u>Mae Hodaka</u>: Class 2 for approx last 1/3rd of climb. 4 hours from Shimazuya Hotel, ascent, 3 hours 30 min descent. 5000 ft of climbing. Clear and warm.

Note: Yaki Dake extremely active on 20th and 25th Sept. Very large fissures noted on northeast and northwest slopes in comparison with previous inspection of original limited fumarole area in Summer 1961. Koyas open during current visit: Hodaka, Karisawa, Yakoo Sanso; Yari-take (summit Koya only) other Koyas are closed at this time of year.

Thomas Lovell Johnston

<u>19th July 1964</u>

It is now 11 years since a climb or climbs have been recorded by an Englishman. (See 10.9.53 Capt. Ashcroft).

On the 19th July 4 very weary men arrived in Kamikochi after travelling

クライマーズ・ブック対訳

2. 奥穂高：クラス2（小屋より上先）。上高地から涸沢（カリサワ）小屋まで4時間半。そこから山頂まで2時間半（穂高小屋から山頂まで20分）。横尾山荘まで下り3時間、そこから上高地まで2時間。曇り、寒い。
3. 奥穂高—西穂高のトラバース：クラス3。5時間。浮き石。
4. 槍：小屋の上の主峰、クラス2（クラス3＆4のルートもある）。上高地から槍小屋まで6時間半。そこから穂先まで20分。下り6時間。快晴、寒い。
5. 前穂高：登攀のラスト約3分の1はクラス2。清水屋（シミズヤ）旅館から登り4時間、下り3時間30分、約1,500mの登攀。快晴、暖かい。

注意：9月20日と25日、焼岳（ヤキダケ）は活動が非常に活発だった。1961年の夏にも、噴気孔がもともとあったあたりを調べたが、今回あらたに北東・北西の斜面に極めて大きな割れ目が認められた。今回の登山中に営業していた小屋：穂高、涸沢、横尾山荘（ヨコオ）。槍岳（山頂の小屋のみ）。他の小屋はこの時期閉鎖されている。

トーマス・ラベル・ジョンストン

1964.7

1964年7月19日

英国人が最後に登攀の記録を残してから11年が経過している（1953年9月10日付、アッシュクロフト大尉の記録参照）。

practically non-stop from Hong Kong. We came to Japan to climb as much as possible and make up for our exile in HongKong. We are all in the Royal Air Force and are members of the R.A.F. Mountain Rescue Team.

SGT   JACK BAINES
S.A.C.   FRANK WARD
S.A.C.   BRIAN KNOTT
S.A.C . ROY PAYN

★   Because of the expense involved it means that camping is our limit for accommodation.

The 19th and 20th of July were spent in resting and organizing. The morning of the 21st (6 am) we ascended Mae-Hodake up the well marked trail then returned to Kamikochi.

22nd July. A late start (noon) to NISHIHO-SANSO. 2 1/2 HRS.

23rd July Early start, after a rice and raw egg breakfast!!! — NISHI-HODAKE, The Gendarmes — OKU-HODAKE — HODAKA-DAKE-SANSO 6 1/2 hours. (There are fixed chain & wire ropes en route, no rope required if competent)

24th July — MT. KARASAWA, — KITA-HODAKE — OKIRRET, MINAMI-DAKE — NAKA-DAKE — OGUI-DAKE(?), YARIGATAKE-SANSO — MT. YARIGATAKE. (10 MIN ↑ 12 MIN ↓) 6 1/2 Hrs.

25th July Return to KAMIKOCHI. 5 HOURS. The weather on the 23rd & 24th was quite cold and very misty. This appears to be the 1st time (in this book) that a Westerner has done the complete ridge.

♥   The ridge is comparable to the Skye (SCOTLAND) Ridge and is truly as good. No snow was encountered. YARI was overflowing with people. There is now a route up and a route down. From the hut (5 am) one can see a living thread of color moving slowly up and slowly down YARI.

26th July 1964. The day was spent 'festering' — washing etc. ASAHI BEER is very good and a walk around the camp-site campfires a must.

クライマーズ・ブック対訳

7月19日、疲労困憊（こんぱい）した4人の男性が上高地に到着する。香港からここまでほとんど休みなしだった。日本に来たのはできる限り多くの山を登り、香港生活の鬱憤（うっぷん）を晴らすためだ。全員、英国空軍に属し、英国空軍山岳救助隊のメンバーである。①

①全員、香港駐在の英国空軍山岳救助隊のメンバーで、上記同様。日本人の歩行、登行時間の平均よりかなり早い。蝶―常念は「丘歩きのレベル」との評も。

　　ジャック・ベインズ軍曹
　　フランク・ウォード上等兵
　　ブライアン・ノット上等兵
　　ロイ・ペイン上等兵

★　経費を考えると、夜は野営するしかない。
　7月19日と20日は休憩と準備に使った。21日の朝（6時）、しっかりと目印のついた前穂高（マエホダカ）の登山道を登り、上高地に戻る。
　7月22日。ゆっくりと出発（正午）、西穂山荘に向かう。2時間半。
　7月23日　朝早く出発。出掛ける前の朝食はご飯と生卵！！！　西穂高（ニシホダケ）、ジャンダルム―奥穂高―穂高岳山荘（ホダカダケ）、6時間半。（途中、鎖とワイヤロープが固定されているので、実力があればロープは不要）。
　7月24日　涸沢岳―北穂高（キタホダケ）―大キレット、南岳―中岳―オオグイ岳（？）②、槍ヶ岳山荘―槍ヶ岳（10分↑、12分↓）、6時間半。

②大喰岳（おおばみ）の読み間違い。

　7月25日　上高地に戻る。5時間。23日と24日は非常に寒く、とても霧が濃かった。欧米人がこの主脈の縦走に成功したのは（この宿帳を見る限り）今回が初めてのようだ。③

③事実誤認。

♥　ここはスカイ島（スコットランド）の峰に引けを取らないくらいすばらしい。雪は見当たらなかった。槍は人であふれていた。今では登りのルートも下りのルートもある。山小屋からは（午前5時）、色の筋がとどまることなく、槍をゆっ

"Danny Boy" and "Clementine" seem to be the favorite.

27th July 1964. 7 am start. AZUMI — CHOGI-TAKE — CHO-TAKE — JŌNEN TAKE. — JŌNEN SANSO (GOYA?). 5 1/2 hours. Guide book time 8 hours?? The hut was just reached in time as a thunder-storm was brewing up.

28th July 1964. Back to Kamikochi. The trip as the whole is a "fell-walkers" route and fairly easy. No ropes etc are needed. Jōnen Sanso is an excellent place and about the smartest we stayed in whilst in Hotake.

29th. We leave for TATEYAMA & TSURUGI for some rock climbing we hope with the famous guide SAHAKI TOMIO.

♠ Although we camped at Kamikochi the staff at the Inn were very hospitable. I even had a "hot spring bath" — Probably looked filthy.

We all enjoyed our stay in Kamikochi and if possible will return again.

JB——
(J. Baines)
Yorkshire Mountaineering Club
Royal Air Force
Junior Mountaineering Club of Scotland (Lochaber Branch)
N.C.O. 1/C R.A.F. KAITAK MOUNTAIN RESCUE. (HONG-KONG).

2. 10. 65 <u>POST SCRIPT</u>
Whilst at Tateyama we climbed, Yatsumine ridge, Oku-DAINICHI, TSURUGI, TATEYAMA (JODEN, ONANJI BESSAN ETC). Also a short rock climb on the N.W. Face of Bessan about Severe standard. On the way to H. Kong, we climbed Fuji-San.

くり上へ、ゆっくり下へと移動しているのが見てとれる。

　1964年7月26日　「腐った」1日で洗濯などをした。アサヒビールがとてもうまい。キャンプ地ではぜひキャンプファイア巡りをしてほしい。「ダニー・ボーイ」と「いとしのクレメンタイン」が人気のようだ。

　1964年7月27日　午前7時出発。安曇―チョウギタケ―蝶岳―常念岳―常念山荘（小屋？）、5時間半。ガイドブックによると8時間？？　危うく激しい雷雨に見舞われるところだったが、間一髪で小屋に到着した。

　1964年7月28日　上高地に戻る。ルートは全体として「丘歩き」のレベルでかなり平易。ロープなども必要ない。常念山荘はすばらしい場所で、穂高にいる間に泊まった中で一番よかったように思う。

　29日　立山、剱に向けて出発、岩稜登攀に挑む。有名な山岳ガイドの佐伯富男に同行してもらいたい。

♠　上高地でキャンプをしたが、宿の人がとてもよくしてくれた。「温泉」にも入れてもらった。よほど汚らしく見えたのだろう。

　全員が上高地での滞在をとても楽しんだ。できればまた戻ってこよう。

ヨークシャー山岳会
英国空軍
スコットランド・ジュニア山岳会（ロッホアーバー支部）
英国空軍上級下士官
啓徳山岳救助隊（香港）
JB――
（J・ベインズ）

1965年10月2日　追記
立山登攀では、八ツ峰、奥大日、剱、立山（ジョウデン、大

④蝶ヶ岳のピークが2ヵ所ともとれるので、別名と思ったか。現在は蝶ヶ岳山荘近くをピークとする。それにしても早足。

⑤前ページ①参照。

⑥不明。似た山名では淨土山があるが。

15th October 1964

A military party (all from the 16th/5th The Queen's Royal Lancers) set out from Hong Kong on the 12th October for the sole purpose of climbing in these Alps. The party consisted of : —

Major   A.E.G. Gauntlett

Cpl.   D. Macinnes
L/C   D.K. Roberts
Trooper W. Cook
Trooper G. Dunn

We arrived in Kamikoche on the 15th October and set up a base camp. On the following day we set out for Nishiho-Sanso where we had a very comfortable night. we took sufficient food to last 3 days which was as well! We are not yet acclimatized to local food.

★   The fine spell of weather broke whilst we were at the hut and the following morning we set out for Nishi-Odaka and Hodaka under very poor conditions. There was a very cold mist with visibility down to 15 yards and later it rained hard and a strong wind sprang up.

We were very grateful that the route was so well marked.

We spent one night in a hut between Nishi-Odaka and Hodaka and on the

クライマーズ・ブック対訳

汝、別山など）に登った。また、距離は短いが別山北西面の岩稜も登攀した。難易度は「Severe」（険しい）。香港に戻る前、富士山に登った。

1964.10

1964年10月15日

10月12日、英国陸軍の登山パーティー（全員が英国陸軍騎兵連隊、第16／第5クイーンズ・ロイヤル・ランサーズ所属）が香港を出発。日本アルプス登攀を唯一の目的とする。メンバーは以下の通り。

　A・E・G・ゴーントレット少佐
　D・マッキネス伍長
　D・K・ロバーツ上等兵
　W・クック騎兵
　G・ダン騎兵

上高地には10月15日に到着し、ベースキャンプを設営する。翌日、西穂山荘に向けて出発。山荘の夜はとても快適だった。3日分の食料を用意しておいてよかった！　まだ誰も日本の食べ物に慣れていない。

★　小屋にいる間に好天の魔法は解け、翌朝、ひどい悪天候の中、西穂高（ニシオダカ）と穂高（ホダカ）に出発した。冷え込みが厳しくなり、霧も出て13m先も見えなくなった。やがて雨が激しくなり、風も強く吹き始めた。

登山ルートには目印がしっかりついていたので、とても助

followed morning ascended the western peak of Hodaka before descending into the valley of Kamikoche.

♥   Today is lovely and fine once again and we have taken advantage by drying out all our kit.

We intend to spend another 4 days in this region. Tomorrow we plan to tackle Yaki — the volcanic mountain to the S.W. of the Hodaka range. After that it is anyone's guess!

A most enjoyable 4 days so far.

****

19 Oct 64

P.S. Yari Daki climbed today. An interesting experience — a lot of loose rock!

2.10.65

Once again I have returned to Kamikochi, with 3 different companions from the R.A.F.

  S.A.C.   Morpett
  S.A.C.   Dales
  S.A.C.   Simon

We arrived in Toyama on the 21st September, and after spending a day

かった。

　西穂高と穂高の間にある小屋①で一晩過ごし、翌朝、穂高の西側の峰に登頂してから、上高地の渓谷に下りた。

♥　今日はまたとてもすばらしい天気になった。好天を利用して、持ち物すべてを乾かすことができた。

　あと4日はここにいようと思う。明日は穂高連峰の南西にある火山、焼岳に挑戦するつもりだ。そのあとはまだ何も決まっていない！

　これまでのところ、最高の4日間だ。

*******※

1964年10月19日

追記：今日、槍岳を登攀。おもしろい経験ができた——浮き石が多かった！

①今は撤去されたが、天狗のコルには避難小屋があった。

※署名か？（判読不明）

1965.10

1965年10月2日

　また上高地に戻ってきた。同伴したのは以前と違う空軍のメンバーだ。

　　モーペット上等兵
　　デイルス上等兵
　　サイモン上等兵

　9月21日に富山に到着。剱登攀に1日、立山登攀に1日

up Tsurugi, and a day on Tateyama, we set off on a 6 day walk to Kamikochi, via Goshiki Sanso, Surgonagoya, TARO Sanso, MITSUMATERENGE-SANSO, YARI-SANSO then Kamikochi. After a day's rest in Kamikochi we went to HOTAKE via KANIZAWA then DAKESAWA.

There is snow on the hills now and a little ice on the northern faces. However for the most part of our journeys we have had superb weather. Kamikochi in the autumn is a really beautiful place.

★ This is most likely my very last time in the Japan Alps as I return in 6 months time to England I will always remember my two holidays in the Japanese Alps, mainly for the mountain scenery and also for the good hospitality offered by the Japanese people. Thank you.

JB——
(J. BAINES)

Monday 11 September 1972

Since my notes herein of July 5th 1947, I have come to know the N. Alps very well, having made scores of trips in the total of 18 years that I have been in Japan since that time. Being now 61, my climbing is slow and painful, but I still love these hills well enough to come anyway. This time, our trip (with my wife of 10 years, Nobuko) was a zigzag, with the various views highly recommended: Nakabusa Onsen, TsubaKuro, DaiTenjo, Higashi DaiTenjo, Yokodosi, Jōnen, Chō, Yokoo, Karasawa, Kita Ho, Minami Dake, Yari, Yari Daira, Shin Hotakta Onsen, up the new (for me!) cable to Nishi Ho

を使ったのち、上高地まで6日間の行程で出発した。五色山荘、スルゴナ小屋①、太郎山荘、三俣蓮華山荘(ミツマテ)、槍山荘を経て上高地というルートだ。上高地で1日休んだあと、カニザワ②、岳沢経由で穂高(ホタケ)に登った。

　現在、山には雪があり、北面には少し氷もある。しかしながら、ほとんどの行程ですばらしい天気に恵まれた。秋の上高地は本当に美しい場所だ。

★　日本アルプスはおそらく今回が最後になると思う。6ヵ月後に英国へ帰国するからだ。これからも、日本アルプスで過ごした2回の休暇を思い出しては、山の景色に加え、日本の人々のすばらしいもてなしを懐かしむことだろう。ありがとうございました。

JB——
（J・ベインズ）

①スゴ乗越小屋と思われる。

②「カニザワ」は不明。

1972.9

1972年9月11日　月曜日

　1947年7月5日に記録を残してからというもの、私は北アルプスにずいぶん詳しくなった。あれから日本での生活も18年になり、その間に何十回となくここを訪れているからだ。現在は61歳で、登山のスピードも落ちて体にこたえるが、それでも訪れてしまうほど、ここの山を愛する気持ちに今も変わりはない。今回の旅は（結婚して10年になる妻のノブコを同伴）あちらこちらをまわり、評判の高い景色をいろいろ楽しんだ。中房温泉、燕、大天井(ダイテンジョウ)①、東大天井(ヒガシダイテンジョウ)、横通

①地元ではオテンショとも呼んでいる。

Sanso, & down to Kami-Kochi. Making all my trips more enjoyable were the friendly people in the huts, most of whom now know me well and welcome me warmly. As in 1947, I would still like to see more attention paid to safety and information in the mountains, to reduce the yearly unnecessarily large number of injuries and deaths. Specifically, there should be many more trail signs, indicating time & distance to the huts. Also helpful would be signs in a large print at all high mountain trail entrances, advising the need for caution and for having all necessary emergency equipment — (rain clothing, flashlight, maps, <u>warm</u> clothing for the high peaks & ridges etc). I should like to extend my thanks here especially to the following families: Kamijo of Tokusawa, Yamada of Yokoo etc., Imada of Hotaka, Koyama of KitaHo, Okida of Minami Dake & Yari Daira, Hokari of Yari, Akanuma Atsuo-san and all his staff members at Enzansō, Kassen, Ōtenjo, & Ōyari.

★   Also, although this book seems to concentrate on the Yari-Hodaka range, I should like to add my thanks & appreciation to all the Saeki and Shitake of the Tsurugi-Tateyama and Kurobe regions.

It has been a pleasure to be allowed to write once more in this volume, the last entry of 5 July 1947 having been my first introduction to the N. Alps, and the present one being written perhaps near the end of my ability to go anywhere in the mountains that I would like to.

チャック・ボーデン   Charles (Chuck) B. Bowden
Tokyo — Shinagawa-Ku, *-*-* Kita Shinagawa / Tel: ***-****

P.S. I would really like to see copies of this "Onsen Ba" made available, even if only mimeographed, and would like to have a copy if they become available.

し、常念、蝶、横尾、涸沢、北穂、南岳、槍、槍平、新穂高温泉、それに、新しい（私にとっては！）ケーブルカーで西穂山荘まで登り、上高地に下りた。小屋の皆さんが気さくなので、旅は一層楽しいものとなった。今ではほとんどの人が私をよく知っていて、温かく迎え入れてくれる。1947年のときと同様、いたずらに多いケガや死亡事故の年間件数を減らすために、ここの山々の安全性や情報にもっと注意を払ってもらいたいと考えている。特に、登山道には小屋までの時間や距離を記した案内板がもっとたくさんあるべきだと思う。それに、標高の高い山なら、登山道の入り口に大きな文字の看板があった方がいいだろう。注意を喚起し、必要な非常用装備（例えば、雨具、懐中電灯、地図、山頂や尾根用の<u>防寒着</u>など）を伝える。ここで次の皆さんには特に深く感謝したい。徳沢の上條家、横尾の山田家ほか、穂高の今田家、北穂の小山家、南岳と槍平の沖田家、槍の穂刈家、燕山荘や合戦、大天井、大槍でお世話になった赤沼淳夫さんとスタッフの皆さん、ありがとうございました。

★　また、この本は槍・穂高連峰が中心だと思うが、剱・立山、黒部一帯の佐伯家と志鷹（シタケ）家の皆さんにも深く感謝したい。

　ここに再び記録を書き残せることになり、うれしく思う。前回の1947年7月5日付の記録は私が初めて北アルプスを訪れたときのものだが、これからは気の向くままに山を歩き回るのが難しくなるだろうから、これが最後の記録になるかもしれない。

チャック・ボーデン②※　チャールズ（チャック）・B・ボーデン
東京都品川区北品川 *-*-*、電話 ***-****※

追記：ガリ版刷りでも構わないので、この「温泉場」の冊子化を深く望む。実現した暁には、ぜひ1冊いただきたい。

クライマーズ・ブック対訳

②チャック・ボーデン氏は相当の日本山岳通とみる。1947年以降、北アに親しみ、北アの山小屋経営者の大半を承知している。

※日本語署名。

※住所、電話番号の詳細が記入してあるが、伏せた。

監修後記

山岳ジャーナリスト　菊地俊朗

　通読して印象に残ったのは、イギリス人が大半であること。特に牧師、軍人、加えて女性の名も目立つ。
　ノートの提案者W・ウェストンが同国人のせいもあろうが、産業革命後、いち早くブルジョアジーが旅の自由を獲得し、旺盛な好奇心、探究心をアルプスはじめ、世界の極地にぶつけていたことが伺える。

　牧師が多いのには訳がある。カナダ人宣教師A・C・ショーが軽井沢の別荘地化の先鞭をつけたが、やがて喧騒してきた軽井沢に嫌気をさした牧師らが、野尻湖畔に新しい別荘村を開設した。夏休み、長期滞在の間に交通の便が進んだ上高地方面に足をのばすようになった。
　戦後は香港駐在の英軍人らが、休暇中にやってきていた。来訪者は異口同音に上高地の自然賛歌を記している。高山のないイギリス人にとって、槍・穂高の景観はアルプスに匹敵するイメージだったようだ。
　夫妻登山も目につく中で、1913年7月、2人の女性が車道開通以前の中房川から有明山→中房温泉→燕を登った記録は知らなかった。日本女性の穂高→槍縦走は、1923年の村井米子（むらいよねこ）が最初とされるが、その10年前から牧師夫人らは槍や前穂に登頂していた。
　欧米人の歩行は速い。登山道が整備された現在でも、上高地→槍ケ岳は日本人だと8時間以上が普通。が、彼らは1～2時間短い。前穂高へは6時間未満で達している。ただ案内した嘉門次らも同タイム。困難な岩場で、「嘉門次の綱に助けられた」との記述があるが、猟師は獲物搬送用などに綱を持参していた。使用法、材質、長さなどは細かく伝承されていない。しかし、記録から判断すると、案内人の体力、技量とも、外国人に互していたのは確かのようだ。
　記録の中での"特注"は、J・M・デイヴィスの1915年6月6日の焼岳大噴火の体験記である。焼岳は明治期末から活動の兆しをみせ、1909年3月末に噴火している。この時、上高地温泉の冬季留守番をしていた嘉門次は、新聞に状況を伝えている。6年後、同温泉に居合わせたデイヴィスは、直後に梓川右岸を温泉から1キロほど下流まで踏査したり、翌日はイカダらしきものをつくり、誕生した池の調査を試み、科学的データを記してい

る。デイヴィスの滞在は6月15日にまで及ぶ。探究心は見上げたものだ。

　鵜殿正雄とともに1909年、前穂→奥穂→北穂の縦走をしたガレン・M・フィッシャーの記録は、6年後に再訪した際、"記憶"として書かれた。それなりに貴重だが、鵜殿の記録と照合すると、一部に記憶違いもあるようだ。

　ノートは外国人の槍、穂高観で、日本側のイメージと若干異なる印象もある。記録は参考文献に値するが、「日本アルプス」の命名者、ガウランドや明治10年代から登山を含む日本各地の外国人向け旅行案内書を発刊したチェンバレン、E・サトウらの名が登場しないのはなぜか。ウェストンの呼びかけによるノートのせいか、知らないせいなのか。

　旧制の高校、大学の山岳部は、明治期末から創部され始めたが、当初は「旅行部」と称した。日本独特の「近代登山」の用語が広まったのは大正期以降で、登山は旅行の一分野と受け止められていた。結果としてウェストンの助言で誕生した日本山岳会創設（1905年）以前の登山行為を、日本人、外国人を問わず"軽視"する風潮を招いた――との疑念を払拭できないでいる。

Editorial Supervisor's Afterword

Toshiro Kikuchi
Mountaineering Journalist

When reading through the book I was impressed by the fact that the majority of writers were British. The names of missionaries, soldiers, and women stood out in particular.

Perhaps this is simply due to the fact that Walter Weston, who provided the notebook, was an Englishmen, but it also suggests how, in the wake of the industrial revolution, the bourgeoisie were quick to gain the freedom to travel, testing their enormous curiosity and spirit of inquiry in the remotest corners of the world.

There is a reason for the prevalence of clergymen. Canadian missionary Alexander Croft Shaw pioneered the development of Karuizawa as a summer resort destination, but missionaries who grew weary of the hustle and bustle there later established a new retreat on the banks of Lake Nojiri. As transportation access improved, those enjoying extended summer stays at Lake Nojiri also began venturing out to the Kamikochi area.

After the war, members of the British military stationed in Hong Kong came to visit while on furlough. Visitors all wrote in praise of Kamikochi's natural beauty. People from Britain, a country without high peaks, appear to have found the scenery of the Yari-Hotaka range comparable to that of the Swiss Alps.

Married couples climbing together also drew my attention, but I had been previously unaware of the July 1913 journey by two women along the route up the Nakabusa River and then from Mt. Ariake to Mt. Tsubakuro by way of Nakabusa Onsen prior to the opening of the roadway. The first Japanese woman to traverse from Hotaka to Yari is said to have been Yoneko Murai in 1923, yet Mrs. Weston and other women from overseas were summiting Yari and Maehotaka a full decade before then.

The Europeans and Americans kept up a good pace, too; most Japanese require more than eight hours to climb from Kamikochi to Mt. Yarigatake even along the maintained trails of today, yet climbers from overseas covered the distance in a full hour or two less. They reached Maehotaka in less than six hours. The guide Kamonji, of course, kept the same pace. One climber writes that on a tricky rocky patch he only "escaped a bad fall" due to the fact that he "had hold of a rope held by Kamonji." As a hunter, Kamonji would have carried rope for use in transporting game, though details such as how it was used, what it was made of, and its length are unclear. Nevertheless, the record suggests that Kamonji was every bit as strong and as skilled as the foreigners he led.

Of special importance among the records is J.M. Davis' tale of his experience during the great eruption of Mt. Yakedake on 6 June 1915. Mt. Yakedake showed signs of activity during the latter years of the Meiji period and erupted at the end of March 1909. Kamonji was serving as winter caretaker at Kamikochi Onsenba at the time and provided newspapers with an account. Davis happened to be staying at the inn during the eruption six years later and wrote, also recording various scientific data, how he immediately explored the right bank of the Azusa River for about a kilometer downstream from the inn before cobbling together a raft the following day to investigate the newly formed lake. He stayed through 15 June, an impressive demonstration of his inquisitive spirit.

Galen M. Fisher's account of his traverse from Maehotaka to Okuhotaka and then Kitahotaka with Masao Udono in 1909 was recorded from memory during a subsequent visit six years later. Although a valuable record in its way, comparing it with the account left by Udono suggests that Fisher may have misremembered some aspects.

The notebook suggests, too, that climbers from overseas see Yari and Hotaka somewhat differently than Japanese do. It is certainly a worthy reference, but one wonders why the names of figures such as William Gowland—who gave the Japanese Alps their name—or Basil Chamberlain and Ernest Satow—who published a series of travel guidebooks for foreigners covering Japan, including its mountains, beginning in the 1880s—make no appearance. Is it because the notebook began as an appeal from Weston? Or were the writers simply unaware of these men?

Alpine clubs (*sangakubu*) were established under the old high school and university system beginning in the late Meiji period. At first they were known as "travel clubs" (*ryokobu*). The uniquely Japanese term "modern mountaineering" (*kindai tozan*) was only popularized during the Taisho period (1912–1925), so mountain climbing before then was considered merely a subset of travel. I cannot shake the suspicion, therefore, that mountain climbing in Japan prior to the establishment of the Japanese Alpine Club in 1905—the result of a suggestion by Weston—tended to be thought lightly of by both Japanese and foreigners alike.

ノートの原文は、執筆された年等から一部は著作権保護期間内の可能性がありますが、執筆者本人や著作権継承者の所在が確認できません。このため、本書は平成28年6月14日に著作権法第67条の2第1項の規定に基づく申請を行い、同項の適用を受けて作成しました。

The publishers of The Climbers' Book have determined that a number of the messages written in the notebook, based on their content and dates, may still be subject to copyright protection. We have, however, been unable to confirm the location of the writers. In accordance with the Copyright Act, we have made the necessary application to the Agency for Cultural Affairs to use such materials in the production of this book.

監修・執筆

菊地　俊朗（きくち・としろう）

　1935 年、東京生まれ。早稲田大学卒業後、信濃毎日新聞社入社。64 年、ヒマラヤ遠征報道で日本新聞協会賞受賞。常務・松本本社代表を最後に退職。現在山岳ジャーナリスト。日本山岳会会員。主な著書に『栄光への挑戦』（二見書房）『山の社会学』『北アルプスこの百年』（文藝春秋）『釜トンネル—上高地の昭和史』（信濃毎日新聞社）『白馬岳の百年—近代登山発祥の地と最初の山小屋』（山と渓谷社）ほか。松本市在住。

三井　嘉雄（みつい・よしお）

　1936 年、長野県生まれ。日本山岳会会員。日本山岳会の年報『山岳』に、4 年間にわたり日付順の「W・ウェストン年譜」を共同執筆。著書に『黎明の北アルプス』。訳書に、英国山岳会が所蔵していた、W・ウェストンによる日本での登山について記した手書きの日記 4 年分を見つけて翻訳し、『日本アルプス登攀日記』として刊行。『日本山岳会百年史』元編纂委員 13 人のひとり。

翻訳スタッフ

　保科京子：英文和訳

　ハート・ララビー　Hart Larrabee：和文英訳

　中村節子：独文和訳

　シルビー・ジャコ　Sylvie Jacquot：仏文和訳

　松本　浩：中文和訳

　ナーガ・インターナショナル：翻訳協力

編集協力

　上高地ルミエスタホテル

　大町市立大町山岳博物館

　牛丸　工

　山浦剛典

クライマーズ・ブック刊行会
　　松本市／アルピコグループ／松本市アルプス観光協会／
　　上高地観光旅館組合／北アルプス山小屋友交会／
　　公益社団法人　日本山岳会／信濃毎日新聞社

刊行事務局・編集
　　信濃毎日新聞社メディア局出版部

装丁
　　近藤　弓子

ウェストンが残したクライマーズ・ブック
外国人たちの日本アルプス登山手記

2016年8月11日　　初版発行
2016年8月25日　　第2刷発行

製作／信濃毎日新聞社
　　　〒380-8546　長野市南県町657
　　　TEL026-236-3377　FAX026-236-3096
　　　https://shop.shinmai.co.jp/books/

印刷／信毎書籍印刷株式会社

製本／株式会社渋谷文泉閣

Ⓒ Committee for the Publication of the Climbers' Book 2016　Printed in Japan
ISBN978-4-7840-7288-0 C0090

定価はカバーに表示してあります
乱丁・落丁本はお取り替えいたします。

本書のコピー、スキャン、デジタル化等の無断複製は著作権法上での例外を除き禁じられています。本書を代行業者等の第三者に依頼してスキャンやデジタル化することは、たとえ個人や家庭内での利用であっても著作権法上認められておりません。